Sleeping With The Lights On

Joe McClain Jr.

DEDICATION

This book is dedicated to the memory of my dear childhood friend Kelsey "Joe" Carter. May you rest in peace and fly high with the angels.

ACKNOWLEDGMENTS

God, my family and all the military personnel who I have had the pleasure to serve with around the world. I hope this book inspires you all to keep reaching for your goals outside of the uniform. #ECSD

1 THE CALL

"You sure you wanna do this man? I mean...this ain't just moving somewhere else across the states. You risking it all to move halfway across the world. In a whole different world for that matter." I sat there and pondered that question for what seemed like eternity.

"Gimme some time to think about it bruh," I replied.

"You got 48 hours man. I can't hold the position forever cause the boss man is on my ass about filling it. Make sure you holla at me in exactly two days."

"Aight bruh, I got you."

"Gone my nigga." The phone hung up on Tony's end as I just held the celly in my hand. He wasn't lying. It was a risk unlike any other that I had ever taken. Stay here in the great city of Las Vegas or take twice the money, which was over 200k per year, and isolate myself on an island for two years. I sipped the last bit of the Hennessy medicine in my glass and waltzed on over to my computer.

Guam. Guam. Guam, I said to myself. I had no idea what this place was or where it was. Thank God for Google Maps though, because I swear it would be a lot of folks in the world lost without it. I typed it in and patiently waited. Finally, it loaded up.

"MAN, I'LL BE DAMNED!!!" I said that shit out loud as I looked at this place. It was a little island, located off the coast of Southeast Asia, in the Marianas Island chain. 30 miles long and 8 miles wide was its brief description. Two U.S. Military bases occupied this land, along with a bunch of jungles. From the pictures that were poppin' up, it looked more like an episode of Animal Safari. I sat back in my computer chair, folding my hands, rocking back and forth with an unsure mindset. I grabbed my mouse, clicked on my documents and started looking at old pictures of what used to be.

There we were. Lamar and Tonya. Former lovers, friends, all of that. We met at a New Year's Eve party thrown by one of the homies years ago. 2009 to be exact. I approached her, but she wouldn't buy into my game. She did however take my number. Eventually she called and our journey began. What started off as a very long conversation turned into almost three years worth of love. Unfortunately, it didn't last. We ended on very bad terms. On her end, it was the additional male figure. On my end, it was a lack of forgiveness. What made it worse is that we were engaged when we decided to call it quits.

Both sides may have played a part, but I blame myself for most of what went down. I still was salty from everything.

We didn't work and it sucked because I had looked forward to becoming married and living the good life of raising a family with a beautiful woman. On the other hand, it was a good thing because her moms didn't like me and I for damn sure didn't have much care for her. I saw exactly why the movie 'Throw Momma from the Train' was made. Some parents try to run their children as adults and it's pathetic. It was already enough dealing with Tonya as my partner. I didn't need to be dealing with additional stress from the momma who wanted things her way. I just shook my head, trying to clear my thoughts. Between relationship failures, not being able to see my daughter in Texas and family problems, I was a complete mess. I was very successful, but I didn't have what I wanted in life. That was simply peace of mind.

I had been in Las Vegas for over a decade, ever since moving here from Detroit. It was the best thing that ever happened to me. Detroit was like walking around in a cemetery. No matter where you were, you saw death at every turn. There was no hope it seemed for the residents of my city, especially us growing up on the East Side. My reason for leaving was much more than that life sucking streets, though. I grew up in a broken home. My moms and pops were married, but they damn sure didn't have a marriage. It was more like two strangers living under the same roof, tolerating each other. The shit I seen when I was younger left a blueprint in my mind that I couldn't get rid of.

I remember the nights my dad would come in drunk, and just start shit for no reason. I remember the random phone calls from women with whom he had cheated on my mom with. My mom, she had her own flaws as well. She was angry inside at herself for a lot of things. However, instead of harnessing that anger, it was taken out on me and my older Sister. In turn, my sister took a lot of her anger out on me. One night when she was fifteen, she even told me that she hated me. As a baby brother, who was only eight years old at the time, it felt like someone stabbed me in the heart and left the knife in there. I never understood it until I got older. My sister and I had a lot of conversations that cleared the air on a lot of things. I just honestly used to sit back and wonder. Why the hell was I even in existence? It seemed like all of my parent's woes were centered around me. That made me wish that Lamar Atteley III was never born.

Time eventually allowed me to put everything in the back of my mind and move on with my life. At age 20, I moved out to Vegas with a friend who had left the D right after we graduated from Finney High School in 2002. It took me an additional two years to join him, seeing that I thought there were brighter days ahead for me at the crib. College though, it didn't work out. I had to drop out of Eastern Michigan University during the second semester of my sophomore year. Money woes, too much partying and a near fatal attempt on my life had me tired of not only college, but the state of Michigan as a whole. I had to make a change.

I was now 27, with my own place, car, benefits, all that. I started off in 2004 as a hotel clerk working in The Riviera Hotel and Casino. It was okay, but I needed much more if I was going to succeed in life. For the next six to seven years, I shifted between work, school and several internships. Now it was 2012 and I was a civilian computer analyst working for the Air Force. There were many tiresome nights as I had to balance my personal life and work. With the help of The

Good Lord, however, I made it through and was carving out a pretty good life for myself. I, however, was on the cusp of another huge decision. Stay where I was comfortable at, or veer into the unknown to take a risk that would see me as incredibly smart or incredibly stupid.

Tony's call was still pondering through my head. It was a lowly Friday evening in March and I had until Sunday to contemplate whether or not I would take the gig. I needed someone to talk to and I knew just where to go. I hopped in my whip leaving Henderson and bounced out towards my aunt's crib over in North Vegas. It was your typical Vegas spring night. It was warm out with a great breeze to soothe your soul. Passing by the strip, I looked at the lights a little differently. They were a little bit brighter than normal. The screens with all their flare and animation seemed to have a greater glow with them tonight. Would this be the last time that I indulged in this amazement? I knew the answer was no, seeing that even if I did go overseas, I could always come back to visit. However, this was home now.

Vegas saved me, as it had for many other people in the world. I knew I wasn't the only one. There was one man in particular from Michigan who had turned this town into his own personal playground. Floyd "Money" Mayweather was a perfect example that no matter what your beginnings were, you do not let it define your ending. He was a major inspiration and I wanted to follow in the legacy of cats making it from the inner city to prosperity. Along with winning in life comes hate. Watching how he dealt with it though, I knew what blueprint to follow.

Some old UGK was going through my speakers as I finally exited off the 95 Freeway towards Ann Road. I was geeked up, as I knew my Auntie April and Uncle Barry would give me the words I needed to hear to make a proper decision. She had moved out here years ago and met my now uncle. It was a perfect match. I had so much love for him just for the simple fact that he gave April a glow like no one had ever seen before. The way I looked at it, if my aunt was happy, then I was happy. I was extremely grateful that Barry was a part of the family.

I pulled up to their house. It was a gracious sized four bedroom on the corner of the block. The sun had set and everything was chill on cool beans mode. I rung the doorbell only to hear that runt dog of theirs, Puddles, barking like she was gonna do something, knowing damn well she wouldn't hurt a mosquito.

"Hey nephew," my aunt clamored as she greeted me with a hug.

"You lucky you called from the freeway cause you know damn well I don't answer my door unless I invite."

"I'm the nephew, though, auntie," as I plopped down on the plush couch in the living room.

"I could give two fucks if you were Samuel L. Jackson." All I could do was laugh. As funny as it sounded, I knew she was dead ass serious. Shit, that's how black folks operated period. If you didn't call before you came over, you took a good chance of not being let in. It would be you and the front door getting acquainted.

"What's up nephew," my Uncle Barry barreled out, coming from the kitchen with an orange juice in his hand, Puddles running towards him.

"Nothin' much unc. I need some advice from y'all, though."

"What's that nephew?" I clasped my hands and leaned forward, trying to get my words right inside of this thick ass skull of mine.

"Is everything alright?," April asked, putting her laptop down.

"Yea auntie. I got offered a two year position making six figures. The only problem is that I gotta move to Guam to get it." She looked at me for a hot second.

"Well what you waiting on?"

"I dunno auntie. I wanted to get y'all take on it. See what y'all think."

"GO!!!," they both said in unison. That shocked the hell out of me. It was like they were rushing me the hell out of Vegas.

"Go have fun nephew. Get your ass out of Vegas for a minute, live in another country and bring ya uncle back one of those Asian women."

"Nigga please," auntie said as she whipped her neck around at unc. "You want yo ass kicked?"

"Baby, you can have me once sideways cooch done."

"Yea nigga, yo neck gone be sideways." I loved them. They knew how to have fun. They knew how to make a marriage last through sheer humor. After subsiding my laughter, I asked my aunt a simple question.

"You think it'll be good for me?"

"Yea Lamar, go get your money. We'll be alright." I looked back over at unc as he sipped that orange juice in his recliner.

"We good nephew. Go make your money. You young. Live it up. We lived ours. Live yours. We'll be here when you get back." It was like they were making the decision for me.

It was a once in a lifetime opportunity, but I just hated starting over. Then as I watched them engage in convo, I immediately thought about something. She came here to start over. Barry came here from New York to start over. Had neither one of them made their individual moves, they wouldn't have met each other. They wouldn't have been married. They wouldn't have been able to show me the example of what a great marriage was. This was all the confirmation I needed.

"Auntie, can I spend the night here? I don't feel like driving back tonight."

"You sure can. If you hungry, you can pull those leftovers out the fridge and eat cause I ain't cookin' shit tonight." I was good with that. The night continued on with random talks, television watching and me rubbing Puddles spoiled ass whenever April kicked her off of her lap. Midnight finally rolled around. Puddles was passed out on her doggy pillow. Those two had retired to their room for the night. All was quiet in the house. I was in the guest room laying down, the glow of the TV lighting up the walls. I started flipping channels, browsing, not really paying attention to anything on. I was almost at the point of dozing off into dream world when I stumbled across HBO. An old episode of Def Jam Poetry was airing. Now I wasn't into this poetry shit. To me, it sounded like some gay shit brothers used to get women. However, David Banner, one of my favorite hip hop artists was on here. I was thinking to myself, *what is this crazy dude doing on this show?* Then he began to spit. The piece was called 'What About Us?'

WHAT ABOUT US: BY DAVID BANNER

The levees broke in
New Orleans and man
It was a shame that
The camera crews and
The national news merely
Whispered our names.
"Mississippi" What about us.
Was it the value of the land,
Or the worth of the man, that
Made you look away, when Katrina
Hit, like "Bam!!!" Celebrities
Weeping in Louisiana streets,
While rubble and destruction still,
In Mississippi, what about us.
Once again, victims of national neglect,
Poor response, choked our hope,
Like a noose around our necks.
The national leaders, left us hanging
Like the day of the tall trees,
While the wind and rain, (pauses)
While the wind and rain erased our
Lives. But most of y'all acted like
You didn't see. How the hell do you expect
Us to be mentally free. What about us.
Where's the healing? The glass ceiling,
That our nation has erected, our children
Not protected, feeling dejected, hanging their
Spirits in shame, because they were born in a place

That's synonymous with pain. Though the weather
Changed, more shit remains the same. We keep
Playing America's fucked up game. What about us.
The constitution guarantees equal protection,
There must be a connection between, what the
government
Says, and what the government does, not do.
The world watches TV and think that with through
building
And that with through repairing, while the effects
Of Katrina are still glaring...what the fuck about us.
What about us, and since nobody else will say it, I will,
MISSISSIPPI!!! What about us.

It detailed the effects of Hurricane Katrina and how America had forgotten, or rather just abandoned the black people of that tragedy. I ain't gone lie, the shit was deep, but the title made me pose another question to myself. What about me? What about my life? I had to decide where I was gonna take charge of it. I cut the TV off and just stared into the darkness for a little while. Guam. Vegas. Guam. Vegas. Guam........Vegas. I pondered back and forth with the same thought until I looked over at the clock. 12:47 a.m. I reached over to the dresser and grabbed my phone to call Tony.

Tony: "You know I'm trying to dream of a beautiful woman at this hour right?"

Me: "I'm down. Tell me what I need to do?"

Tony: "Meet at the office Monday. 10 o'clock. Conference room."

Me: "Cool."

Tony: "Gone."

That was easier than I thought. However, that feeling of ease quickly dissipated as I thought to myself, *what in the good hell did I just do?* I just accepted a position halfway across the world, in a foreign land, with foreign people. About ten minutes later, I got a text from Tony.

"Just contacted boss man. He is on board and just sent your profile to the folks on the G. You out in two months playboy. Holla at you Monday."

Damn, that was quick. This nigga was not playing when he said he had to have an answer. Man, this shit was really happening. I continued to stare into the darkness. A decade ago, I came to Vegas to make something of my life. Now I would be leaving Vegas to enhance it even more. I could do nothing but smile at this point. Yea, I was a little bit scared and nervous. Deep down though, I knew that everything would be alright. I rolled over, threw the thick ass comforter over my head and drifted off into dream world.

"Sleepyhead!! Wake yo ass up. Breakfast ready."

"Auntie, you ain't gone bring me breakfast in bed?"

"Yea keep waiting nigga." That early morning laugh is what I needed as April turned right back around and walked out the room. I continued to lay down, enjoying the comforts of this bed. That was until Puddles brought her happy pappy ass in there and started licking my face. I swear if I wasn't an animal lover, I would've choked that dog and sent her to Hong Kong.

I got up to brush my teeth. This Saturday morning, it felt a little bit different. It felt unlike any other time that I would brush. For some reason, I felt like a king while doing it. The feeling of excitement overwhelmed me as I scrubbed my gums a little bit harder. I took a good shot of Listerine and swished it around a little longer than usual. Yep, I was indeed feeling myself. I joined my aunt and uncle in the dining room. Auntie had thrown down something serious: grits, biscuits, scrambled eggs, mackerel patties, toast, sausage and bacon. I mean when you got two forms of swine, you know it's gonna be a good day.

"So y'all," as I stuffed a fork full of scrambled eggs smothered in syrup in my mouth. "Last night, I accepted the position."

"Good, good," Auntie said. Unc just nodded his head, seeing that his mouth was full of one of April's buttermilk biscuits.

"When you leaving nephew?"

"Supposedly May, Unc."

"Alright now. Don't forget to send ya Unc one of those sideways coochies."

"Nigga you want ya dick cut off?" As April grabbed a knife and pointed it at him, we all burst out into laughter. As the breakfast continued on, I sat back and analyzed everything. As they talked, I went into my own little dream world. It was March, but May seemed like it was only a day or two away. Here I was enjoying Vegas with my family. Next, I would be on a plane over the Pacific. I had to get

some more advice on this major move and I knew just who
to get it from.

"Yeaaaaa!!! Butler!!!" That was my man Jay Hall,
greeting me

as I entered into his domain. Las Vegas Athletic Club is
where the over sized Hulk type brothers worked out. I had
met this dude a few years back when he moved out here after
finishing a five year stint in the Marine Corps. Not only was
he cool to be around, but he always did his own thing and
that was something I could respect. In today's world, you
always found people trying to be something that they
weren't, all for the sole purpose of fitting into the crowd. This
is why I hung with this dude. I never had to worry about
getting into some negative shit. I knew whatever we did, it
would be something where living on our own terms
determined the amount of fun.

"So man," as he grunted through a cross cable routine.
"Where in the good hell are you going again?"

"Guam bruh." He slammed the cables as he finished up
his set. He stepped over to me 'til we were face to face and
put his finger in my chest.

"Go over there and take that shit over. The same way you
bout to take over this set. Take that bitch over." That was Jay.
Like me, he didn't make excuses. As I cringed and grunted
doing these heavy ass cable sets, with Jay yellin' at my ass to
get that shit, I had a flashback to sum everything up as to
why I should leave.

2 DEATH AT THE DOOR

It was 2006, and I was back in the D visiting family. The trip started off like any other trip. A nigga got off the plane to an awaiting family member. As with most people who leave home and come back, you stop at an eating joint that you can only get back at the crib. For me this time, it was Louie's. I swear on everything I loved they had the best food in the D. Me, I always got the ham and cheese omelette with a side of corned beef. I thought everything would be normal like always. Get in, get my food and get back to the house.

"A nigga, you still getting the same shit or has that West Coast fucked up your appetite?"

"NIGGGGGGGGGGGGGGGGGGGGGGGGGGGGGGG GGA PLEASE!!!!!!!!!!!!!!!!!!!!" I said that shit with emphasis as my cousin, Edward, a.k.a. "Cream Puff," actually had the nerve to play me.

"A well, you know, I thought that Vegas life may have flipped you. You need to bring some of those West Coast bitches out here nigga." I just laughed at him, reminding him that he didn't need any more females, seeing that he was the human pussy slayer around the city of Detroit. I mean, this nigga here, he was a hound. He was the one who taught me how to be a hound, him and his brother Terrell.

When I was sixteen, cuz scooped me up one night when my parents were out of town. We started off blazing a few blunts before hitting the Finney vs. King football game. After watching them niggas go at it, with King pulling out a 28-26 win, we then rolled the town up like some Cali Kush. From Northland Bowling Alley, to Belle Isle, to the Go Kart joint, we were on it. We were high and drunk as shit, but we were definitely on it. Long story short, he met this bad bitch named Juanita who was visiting from Canada with one of her homegirls. We got to the Big Boy burger joint across the street from Belle Isle. Ol' girl I was rappin to was down, until her punk ass square ass dude came in trying to play captain save a hoe. To avoid confrontation, cuz simply wrapped things up, dropped me off at the crib and proceeded to go meet Juanita wherever the hell she was. He beat the breaks off that shit as I figured, ensuring that he gave me play by play the next time he seen a brotha like it was a Pistons vs. Bulls game. Ahh, the memories I tell you.

"Nigga, it's good to have you home man. Real shit."

"Thanks cuz." That made me feel good as we got our bags of food and headed towards the door so we could go back to his crib and indulge. Just as Edward was pushing the door open, some nigga came running towards the door.

POP, POP, POP, POP, POP, POP, POP, POP!!!
Gunshots were flying. I didn't even know exactly how many
or what. I didn't know if we were the ones getting shot at or
what because everything was happening so fast. All I
remembered were loud noises, glass shattering and us
dropping to the deck like sailors at boot camp. As the smoke
cleared, I heard Edward yelling out my name.

"LAMAR!!! LAMAR!!! LAMAR!!!"

"I'M HERE CUZ!!! YOU GOOD??" I looked up, seeing
nothing but blood and glass everywhere. I wasn't sure if it
was my blood or my cousin's. He raised his head up, locking
eyes with me. He had much life in them, so either he hadn't
been shot, or the adrenaline running through his body had
him not feeling anything. We were totally blacked out to the
screams coming from inside the restaurant. Just then, as I
tried to raise up, I felt a heavy weight on my legs. I didn't
know what it was. I figured the worst had happened. I had
been wounded and now I couldn't feel my legs. I was
paralyzed. The burning sensation would come any minute in
my upper body I believed.

"Mar!!!??? Lamar!!!???," as Edward lifted himself up and
wrapped his arms around my upper torso. "It's a dead nigga
on top of you." Cuz pulled me up, as my face began to turn
at the sight of this young brother I saw. My clothes were
bloody as hell, but this nigga was bloody, dead and full of
holes. Ed stumbled and lost his balance as he lifted me,
crashing into the wall.

"Ah shit, you good?," he asked me, out of breath like a
muthafucka.

"Yea," I responded, clearly distraught. Edward started to
pat himself down.

"I don't think I'm hit. You?" I patted myself down, rubbing and feeling everywhere, making sure I wasn't missing anything.

"Naw, I'm good." We were good physically. Mentally, we were messed up. We then just stood there, looking over some good ass food that was spilled and a dead body. Man, this young brotha couldn't have been no more than 21 from the looks of it. His Jordans, half off his ass jeans, Pistons jacket, chain and Red Wings fitted cap was worthless now. It's obvious he wasn't killed for his gear, as all of his shit was still on. What he did, I don't know. I do know, though, that he had now fell victim to these Detroit streets like so many people had before him.

"C'mon Mar. Let's roll the fuck up outta here." We stepped over this young man, the broken glass and headed out the door, trying to become immune to what we just saw. That was one of the reasons that I left the D. It was to save my life. Now I felt the same way about going to Guam. I had to save my life. How would it be saved this time? To answer to that question for you, I had no idea.

"Jay, how'd you handle that change on deployment with those Navy cats? You know, hoppin' from country to country every few weeks or so." I asked him this as he was cranking out 255 on the decline press like it was absolutely nothing. He said nothing. He was fully locked in on his set. I was over him acting as a spotter, even though I damn well knew he didn't need one. As he racked the bar and got up, he looked at me with a look that only he could give.

"Bruh, you just adapt. Change is something you have to deal with. You can either bitch about it, or you can embrace it. Trust me, you'll be good. Now, it's your turn." He was a straight chaser, no bullshit, and I could appreciate that. I jumped on that decline bench, gripped that bar and proceeded to lift. I wasn't as strong as him, but I could hit this a good eight times. As I came down, I took each lift as if it were my life. Inhaling represented me taking in everything that was happening. Exhaling while pushing this shit out represented me pushing out excuses and bullshit. My dude was right. There was no time for excuses. I had to embrace this change. I wasn't a child anymore so the bitching, moaning and complaining could not accompany this move.

I accepted the position and it was time to prepare for the unknown the best way I could. Much like this gym, I was getting GAINZ. The same way you enhance your body in the gym, it's the same way you enhance your own individual life. GAINZ are nothing more than progress, and I was definitely making that. I got home that early evening around 4:30. I was sweaty and tired, but I had a sense of fulfillment. I felt ready to make this move. As I plopped on my couch, I cut on the TV. After all the commercials, including one for an upcoming Money Mayweather fight, on came an old episode of Martin. This was my favorite show of all time. I could sit here and laugh my ass off all day to this. Today though, a certain episode was on that hit me like never before. It was the episode where Martin went to the temple to find himself. As funny as it was, it was also very serious. The lesson I took from it is that you gotta go search for your purpose sometimes, even if everyone else doesn't understand your journey. I cut the TV off and pondered over what I had just saw. I felt this was God telling me that I had to do this. I got up, fixed my protein shake, showered up and headed to bed. It was early, but a lot was going on inside of my head. I needed the rest.

The month of April came around full force. I had let my landlord know that I would be moving out at the beginning of next month. I wanted to simply enjoy the remaining time that I had not only in Vegas, but in the states in general. It was April Fool's and one of the homies was throwing a lil kick back party at Carnival Court next to Harrah's. I slid through in some simple blue and white Forces, jean shorts and a Beast Mode T-shirt. This was the cool thing about this place. It gave you the feel of Vegas without having to dress up to a T. Trust, I enjoyed throwing on the gators, lizard skins, suit, tie and all that when I stepped out. It wasn't too many fools who could touch me in the grown man game. However, it felt good every once in a while to just be loose.

The stage was poppin' as I walked up in this joint, looking for my man Gump 5000. His name was J.T. but we called him Gump. Why was that his nickname? I had no clue. That's how I was introduced to him when I first met him so it stuck. I strolled through looking for my guy, head turning every five feet at the sight of another group of women. It was a gang of white girls in here, ol' high quality ass snow bunnies. I didn't start peepin' them out until I moved out here. It seemed like they were always the ones who were out and about. I loved my sisters but I would not hesitate to go jump in a tub full of snow.

"Ahh shit. Look what the fuck the spirits done drug up in this muthafucka!!!" I turned around towards the direction of that voice.

"GUMP NIGGA WHAT'S POPPIN??!!" I walked over and dapped him up. From the look on his face and the amount of liquor sitting on his table, I could tell that half of his liver was already disintegrated. I sat on down, choppin it up with him and the bruhs chillaxing with him. Eventually, my black ass would get started on the drinking tip as I told the sexy big booty waitress to bring me a shot of Patron. I sat there just enjoying life. It was truly refreshing to be enjoying my last moments in the states with good people. I couldn't do this shit back in the D as someone would've shot some shit up by now. As we all got caught up in the on-stage band doing a rendition of The Roots 'What They Do', I flashed back to the last time I was gathered around a table like this back home. *What they do............. What they do..............That's what I wondered.*

I was sixteen. My parents were into one of their usual arguments. I swore I wish they would have both gotten a divorce years ago. Being trapped in a house without any love, it was the worst thing you could ever imagine as a child. This shit went on for years and years. I couldn't count on love from inside my own four walls, so all I had left in my mind was the streets and my grandmother. I stayed inside of my room hearing their words but I was immune to the whole situation. I hated my father. It was a lot of bullshit he pulled in his time that he thought no one noticed. My whole goal was to grow up and be nothing like him. Did I love him? Yea simply because he was my father, although my relationship with him was more of a toleration. The best thing in my life was getting away from him.

My mom, well, like I said earlier, she was full of a lot of anger. I wish she would've left his ass years ago but there was no budging on her part. There were excuses and that was it. It carried on into the latter years when me and my sister were out of the house as well. How could she stay living in a miserable situation? It beat the hell out of me and it severely used to stress me out. Any who, they were going at it like I said. After a good 20 minutes and hearing my name being brought up at least 20 times, I barged into the next room.

"I'M SORRY!!! I'M FUCKING SORRY!!! I'M FUCKING SORRY I WAS BORN!!!" I can't even remember exactly what happened after I said that except an eerie silence in the house with my cries providing the only noise. I honestly thought they didn't care and I still feel like that at times to this day. The Roots said 'Never do what they do' in one of their songs. That was my life motto growing up in that house on the East Side. Never do what they do because it leads to nothing but bullshit and pain.

"Nigga? Nigga? You good?" Gump was tapping the hell outta me but I was so zoned out that I completely was immune to him.

"LAMAR!!!???" I popped back into the real world.

"Oh shit man, sorry. I zoned for a minute." I grabbed a shot of Patron they had brought to the table and inhaled it while Gump just chuckled.

"Well whatever you was thinking of, let that shit go man. I don't need you in deep thought bout some old booty or whatever at my party." He was right. This wasn't the time to think about old memories that reminded me of the bad days. I was here to cut loose and enjoy myself. We finished up our drinks, chopped it up a little bit more and we left to walk on down to New York, New York. Man, the strip was beautiful this April Fool's night. I guess since I was about to leave, it became a jewel in itself. It was crazy, I tell you. My life was representative of these lights. Bright and vibrant. My soul was representative of the city as a whole. It was great with a dark side that no one wanted to ever see. The mobs were big down here and the asshole side of me was like the mob. If you didn't bring it out of me, there were no worries. However, you cross me and I had to get revenge. That was my achilles heel. Vengeance was something that I needed to let out of my spirit but it was hard. I wanted to not love my parents because I felt they didn't love me. I wanted my ex fiancee to feel the pain that I felt she had caused me. I was just a tit for tat person. You do any wrong to me and I would get you back ten fold. I know it wasn't the Godly thing to do, so all I could do was pray that one day the spirit inside of me would be out of my soul forever.

Just earlier in the year, I had flown down to Texas for someone who had almost hurt one of my female family members. Crazy thing is when I dropped her off at school one day, I saw him and circled his car. She asked me not to do anything and out of respect, I maintained my cool. My big bruh D called me and told me to be careful, reminding me that I was down there in unfamiliar turf. I understood that, however, when you're on a mission, it's hard to stop. That's how nutty I was at times. I needed to chill on that before it cost me dearly one day. We got to New York, New York. Most of the crew was halfway on their way to drunk as a skunk city. My few shots of Patron didn't do much so I was sober enough to keep an eye on everybody.

"Yeaaaaaaaaaaa!!!" That was Jay Hall greeting Gump as we all strolled up to the Coyote Ugly joint that he was a bouncer at. Him and Gump were like Batman and Robin. They were more than brothers. Me and Jay were tight, but those two were on a whole 'nother level. It was like two ninjas with superpowers 'cause they seemed to always be doing some extraordinary stuff.

"Y'all get up in here and get ugly. **Yeaaaaaaa!!!**" That was typical Jay Hall with his "Yea" trademark. We were the only brothers in this place. I had never been in one of these joints. I seen the movie on TV, but I didn't think places like this actually existed.

"ALRIGHT COYOTES.............MAKE IT RAIN!!!" Once the white girl from behind the bar shouted that on the mic, all the women on the bar got to blasting water on everyone. As water hit us all, I just took in the surroundings. Everything slowed down dramatically as if I were strung out on some powerful weed. White boys of course were just looney tooney and enjoying this. Fist pumps filled the air as water flowed. One of the bartenders grabbed a guy by his tie, wrapped her legs around his neck and poured a drink in his mouth. This was great, but my head wasn't too much into it. Gump told me not to be thinking about anything else while I was partying with him but a brother couldn't help it. In a little over a month, I was out of here. No more fun times like this. No more of my guys that I knew. I would have to get a whole new crew or just run dolo while I was over there.

"HEY YOU....BEASTMODE!!!" The fine ass sister on top of the bar had the mic and was looking dead at me. Gump and these fools were going nuts along with everyone else. I pointed to myself as if I didn't know she was talking to me.

"YEA YOU!!! OH...YOU'RE SHY??? HEY EVERYBODY, GET BEAST MODE'S ASS UP HERE!!! BEASTMODE! BEASTMODE! BEASTMODE!!!"

The crowd soon followed as these fools started pushing me towards the bar. I liked how they were chanting my name. It reminded me of what happened when I laid this pipe of mine. I had to fight through a slew of drunk white dudes giving me high fives and yellin in my face. As soon as I got in her reach, she grabbed me by my collar and held the mic out to her side.

"Let's see how much of a beast you are," she whispered. **"HEY GUYS, DO WE THINK HE'S A BEAST?"** The crowd erupted in a roar. I wanted to slap this white boy who had locked his hands on my shoulder and started shaking me uncontrollably, but I just went along with everything. She grabbed two bottles of I don't know what the fuck and just started pouring. She kept pouring and pouring and pouring. Liquor was running all down my shirt. I didn't know what this shit was, but it was good and sweet. Time went in even slower motion then. The vibration of stomps and yells pulsated throughout my body. The turn up was real and the send off was official. However, there was only one send off that could make my departure official.

"A NIGGA........HOW YOU FEEL??" That was Gump as he grabbed me, shook me and was more hype than a pig finding a bucket of shit.

"Man........I'm going back to Detroit."

"WHAT THE HELL ARE YOU TALKING ABOUT MAN?? I ASKED HOW YOU FEEL, NOT WHERE THE FUCK YOU GOIN!!! NIGGA YOU FUCKED UP!!!" Laughter erupted from me, him and the rest of the crew. Crazy thing is that I wasn't fucked up. I was dead ass serious. It was time to go home. It was time to face the D once again. How would it play out? A brother had no idea whatsoever.

3 WELCOME TO HELL

Jay-Z, quite possibly the greatest rapper of all time, had a line in a song titled "You Don't Know." It went, "but this is worse than the Dow Jones/your brains are now blown/all over that brown Brougham/one slip you are now gone/Welcome to hell where you are welcome to sell." That exactly summed up the D right there. It was hell. You could also sell any and everything here to ensure your survival. Like any other crumbling city that selling involved drugs, prostitutes and all kinds of other illegal shit. Hell, if you lost your soul in the city, there would be someone on some random street corner selling it back to you for a dirt cheap price.

My plane landed at the airport on that April 11th day of 2012. It was 2:03 in the afternoon. Here I was, back in the city that bred some of the biggest names you ever heard of in your life; Eminem, Proof, The Bad Boys Pistons, Big Meech,

Maserati Rick, The Chambers Brothers, The Fab Five, Jerome Bettis and many more. Yea, there were a lot more drug dealers than athletes, but that's just how things operated out here. I didn't tell my parents I was coming home. I was gonna surprise them with the news along with other members of my family. I got my luggage and went through hell with HERTZ after their system crashed. After forty-five minutes of waiting and dealing with this crazy customer service clerk who had no customer service skills at all, I finally got my keys and headed out to the rental lot. I seemed to be walking forever and then I finally came upon my vehicle. It was a 2013 Buick Regal. The thing actually looked pretty stylish. Coming up, I could only remember Buicks having a big body, big ass rims and crazy ass paint jobs. All the Dope boys had em. To a youngin on Detroit's East Side, they were like God, and the actual God was second because we seen more souped up whips around our parts than divinity.

I threw my bags in the trunk and proceeded to enter the vehicle. I started it up with a million thoughts running through my head. Memories were an emotional roller coaster here. Unfortunately for me, there were more bad ones than good ones. I took off towards the exit of the lot. I gave my papers to the clerk inside of the booth. No words came from him. There was just a stone cold look at me, the papers, then he handed them back and let the gate up. Yep, I was definitely back home. People swore everyone was their enemy out here. I peeled out, window halfway down, taking in the nice springtime breeze. It smelled like home. This was far from the muggy mountain air of Vegas. Pollution was back in the air. I kept it simple with this drive. Doing a quick trip through downtown, I cruised slowly past Hart Plaza, admiring the giant fist built in remembrance of the great Joe Louis. That huge fist symbolized everything about the people of this city. Strong, fierce, resilient and knock you in your muthafuckin face if you cross us type of mentality. I was proud to be from here, but I knew I couldn't stay here if I wanted to expand. I finally started my way towards the crib off Warren and Chalmers. The closer I got, the more memories started to unfurl inside of my cranium. Every little sight gave me chills; the gas station, the liquor store, the addicts hanging out in droves. Yep, this was the D. I finally pulled up to the house right across from my alma mater. It seemed like yesterday that I was roaming the halls, spitting game to girls and slaying 'em in my basement when my parents were gone to work. I shut the car off in our gravel lot. A lot had changed since I had left the last time. A few houses that were standing some years back were now boarded up. The liquor store even seemed dead. As a kid, I swore it was a concert there 24/7 because it seemed mofos were always outside of there no matter what time of day it was.

The sky was more than clear. It was a little past three and I was still in awe of being back due to the circumstances. I popped open the trunk to retrieve my bags. As I grabbed 'em, I looked to the left. In the distance, there was a wino walking down the street with a dusty trench coat, moving his hands as if he were having a conversation with himself. As I whipped my head to the right, I caught a young man in a black hoodie riding a bike that was too small for his grown behind. We locked eye contact with each other as he slowly cruised by, looking at each other with the "who the fuck are you" stare. I followed him to the corner as he slowed down to look back. He flashed "them rakes" at me and then sped off down the next block. It was the prelude it seemed for some good ol' fashioned hood drama and I for damn sure wasn't interested in that. I slammed the trunk and walked up to the door, ringing that dusty doorbell of ours. How does a doorbell become dusty? I have no idea. Only in the hood I guess.

"Boy what the hell you doing here?" That was my mama, looking like she had seen the IRS man.

"Surprise Ma. I'm home." While I'm smiling, she was steady giving me a happy, yet shocked look. I walked on in, dropped my bags and we embraced in a huge hug. It was good to hold my mom, no matter what we had been through.

"You eat?"

"Naw. I'm a get some Louie's tonight. You want some?"

"Naw, I cooked," she said as she took the smallest duffel bag I had and put it in the dining room. I walked into the kitchen and quickly put to rest the notion of Louie's anything. Moms had chitlins, black eye peas, greens, cornbread and some fried chicken wings.

"Dang Ma. What made you cook all this?"

"Hell, I didn't cook nothing but those wings and that cornbread. All the rest of that stuff was frozen in the deep freezer from Christmas." I should've figured. My parents were good for that. I didn't mind though. It was good to have a bomb ass meal like that upon returning home. Mom sat down at the kitchen table, doing a puzzle as she always did. I heated up a plate full in the microwave and sat down with her. Things were silent for the most part. It was nothing awkward, seeing that my mom really loved her puzzles. I however really wanted us to connect, seeing that this was the last time I would see her in two years.

"So mom, what's been going on?"

"Nothin," as she stayed focused on her puzzle.

"Well….ummm….I took a job overseas for two years. I'm leaving next month."

"Where?," eyes steady focused on that puzzle book.

"Guam. It's a little island somewhere in the Pacific. They paying me literally three times what I make here and it's temporary. I'll be back in two years like I said." She put her pen down and looked dead at me.

"Is that what you want?"

"Yea," I responded hesitantly, thinking she would be upset.

"Alright then. Just send mama some money." I chuckled as she went right back to doing her puzzle.

It was crazy how my family operated. Most families, when they are about to lose a family member to a move of some sorts, would be planning going away parties, be in somber moods or trying to hold on to every bit of the person until they were gone. Not my family. When I say my family, I mean the whole Atteley clan. We were raised to get educated, get out and carve our own way in the world. Besides a few of my peoples who stayed in the city, the rest of us graduated, left off to another state and continued our life. We weren't one of those families that had to be on top of each other every minute of the day. We had phones, e-mail, skype, all that. When we came together for reunions, it was love. However, we didn't overly miss each other because we were all busy carving out our own paths in life. Some of us were in Indiana, California, Alabama, Ohio, Mississippi,

Texas and a few more states. You name the place and we were most likely there in some form, shape or way.

I finished my meal and went off to my room. I plopped on the bed and just stared at the ceiling for a good minute. *POP!!! POP!!! POP!!!* I couldn't tell if those were gunshots or some kids lighting off fireworks three months early. Whatever it was, it wasn't unusual around here. I thought about so much being back here. The journey that I had been through to get to this point in my life right now. It was a long and strenuous one, but I had made it. I found the remote and cut on the 27-inch bubble screen that was still in my room after all these years. Flipping through the channels, I came across TV One. They were showing old episodes of Versus and Flow. Again, I wasn't a fan of this art form. Occasionally though, some inspirational words would come across and change your thinking process.

They introduced a young lady by the name of Brianni Blue out of Oakland. She was a beautiful lady, but her strength amazed me. I say that because she waltzed out on stage pregnant. She had to be close to delivering this baby, because it looked like she was carrying the boulder they rolled in front of Jesus' tomb. Plus, anyone who knows a woman who is pregnant, knows that it takes major strength to do everyday things while a hungry mouth is inside of them kicking away and probably doing pull ups on their intestines. Matter of fact, I had a homeboy who had a two year old we called 'Scooby.' This was the strongest little kid I ever seen. I swear he could pull hummers. He looked like a mini version of Flesh-N-Bone from Bone Thugs-n-Harmony as well.

Any who, I really didn't pay attention to her words. I was really in awe of her strength. One thing I learned in my time is that you have to sometimes be strong for yourself. Everyone won't always be there to hold you or pat you on the back. You literally have to sometimes be everything you need. I learned that from her. That baby didn't stop her. She did what she had to do to deliver a message. No bitching, moaning or complaining. She just did it. I went in and out of sleep until I eventually dozed off for good.

"When you get here boy?" I woke up groggy as hell, not knowing who was talking to me. Once my eyes got adjusted, I seen it was my dad.

"Surprise," I said ever so dead to the world.

"Ya mama told me you goin' to Guam."

"Yea. They offered the job and I took it. How you feel about it?" Dad gave me that nigga please look.

"What it matter what I think? You a grown ass man. You make ya own decisions." I forgot who I was dealing with. I had to remember these weren't parents who were gonna try and talk you out of something. If you wanted to do it, then gone head. Dad walked out the room while I still was sprawled out. I turned over to look at the clock. 8:09 p.m. Damn. I had damn near slept this first night away. It was still early in my book, seeing that I was still in a West Coast time mind state. I couldn't go back to sleep, so I did the only thing I could think of. I called my cuz Edward up.

Edward: "Waddupdoe?"

Me: "A cuz, I'm at my mama and nim house right now."

Edward: **"NIGGA YOU LYIN!!!"**

Me: "Come scoop me fool?"

Edward: "Be there in 20 my nigga."

Me: "Gone."

I honestly had to get out and see my fam. Hell, I had to just get out period. I know Eddie would provide the perfect entertainment for me. I went to the bathroom for a quick wash up. I didn't expect to be doing nothing extraordinary tonight, so there was no need for an all out get fresh session. Soap the armpits, soap the nuts, deodorize and baby powder up, and I was straight. Don't act like y'all ain't did the shit before. I waited by the door, looking out for when cuz was gone pull up.

"Where you going this time of night?" I turned around to see my mama had came up out of her room. I swear she had reminded me of my grandma with that scarf, dusty robe and old house slippers that looked like they had been dragged from L.A. to New York.

"Edward coming to pick me up. We gon hang for a bit."

"Dang.....you just got here. Why don't you chill out?"

"Ma.....,"

HONK HONK. That was Eddie.

"I'll see you later Ma. **Love you!!!**" I shouted that as I shot down the stairs.

"Call me every now and then!!!" I wasn't even tryna hear her as I darted into the car. I loved my mom, but I was grown, and I swore she was still acting like I was a sixteen year old boy in high school headed to a crosstown rival basketball game. Daddy ain't even bother me. He just let me do me.

"What's good nigga?," Eddie said as soon as I shut the door behind me.

"Shit, nothin much mane." We peeled out, headed off to get into whatever we were gonna get into. We had some slaughterhouse blastin as cuz fired up a blunt to ease his senses and aromatize the air.

"Wanna hit cuz?"

"Naw bruh. I can't take no chances with this new joint I just got. Ain't tryna get hired and fired on the same day."

"That's cool with me," as he took another puff of the blunt.

"Shit we gon head to get some gyros real quick and head over to Crystal's house." Man, that was music to my ears. This is why I loved the Midwest. The damn food was on point. I hadn't had an official gyro in years. We had an area out here called 'Greek Town' so you know it was official. I hadn't tasted a better one since I left. Of course, you got some foods that do have exceptions. I thought Detroit's Mexican food was hittin'. That's until I made one of my rounds to Southern California some years back and had a taste of some official Mexican food. I ain't give a fuck where you were from. If your Mexican food wasn't from SoCal, your city's Mexican food wasn't shit. We swung by, got our grub and headed off to the West side to our cousin Crystal's house.

Time was going by slow, which was a good thing. I wanted to just marinate on this whole hometown experience. As we both indulged in these sloppy, yet fire gyros on the road, I couldn't help but notice the little shit. The trash on the side of the freeway, a dead dog, shit like that. I was wondering would that island be the same way. I was thinking too much I know, but it's what I did better than anyone. THINK. If only more people would do it, their situations would be a lot better. We pulled up to the house where Crystal and a gang of our cousins were on the steps chillin'.

"A cuz, I'll be right up. I gotta roll up a few mo!!!" I just laughed.

"Aight cuz." I got out and Crystal's loud ass just started shouting as she ran up and hugged me. It felt great to be back here. We made it to the porch with Nikki, Wanda and a lot more of my crazy family. Being on the porch in the D, with a night time breeze and pure quietness except for your family was rare. With all the craziness out here, no one wanted to even be outside. After a good minute or two, we all started to migrate inside.

"**A Eddie! C'mon!!!,**" I shouted, as I jacked open this ragged ass screen door. Then, I heard a car coming down the street at a fast rate of speed. I turned around, only to witness this black tinted out car coming to a screeching halt right to the side of Eddie's car. I was stunned silent. My eyes were big and my body was fixed. Time had literally stopped. That's when I saw the chopper come out. The flash from the barrel illuminated the night sky. The rattling sound beat through my cardrums as I dove into the house. I covered my head as the shards of glass crashing and metal thumping rung through my eardrums ever so violently.

"**EDDIE!!!,**" I screamed. "**EDDIE!!!**"

It was like there was a demon in my voice. The car screeched off and everything got silent again. I rolled around on the floor, looking at my other family members sprawled out on the floor, not knowing what in the good hell was going on. I was so fucked up that I hadn't even realized Crystal ran out the house screaming Eddie's name.

"**NOOOOOOOOOOOOOO!!!,**" I heard Crystal shouting from outside. We all shot out the door. My cousins were ecstatic. I was fucked up. Nikki yanked the car door open and Eddie's body just slumped out. There were no signs of life. I couldn't even bare looking at him for more than those two to three seconds. I just clasped my hands over my head and walked off. The commotion was beyond loud and crazy as neighbors started to file outside. Some were on their phones and others were just in disbelief. I just sat on the steps ballin' tears, not even trying to imagine what I had just seen. I looked up to life going in slow motion. Neighbors were grabbing my family members, consoling them. Crystal was holding on to Ed's lifeless body in her arms, shirt covered in blood as if she had been shot multiple times. I seen the fire trucks, police and ambulance coming up the street, rolling slowly because the street was flooded with hysterical people in and outside of my family. The lights brought life to this helpless, dim lit block with only two street lights that worked. Except this time, with the bringing of life, another life had ended.

I didn't know how to feel. My phone was ringing like crazy in my pocket, but I ain't even look to see who it was. I watched in full force as caution tape was applied to the trees. A sheet was placed over my cousin's body only after my other cousins pried Crystal away from his body. I couldn't even fathom what was going on. I stared at everything with no life in my eyes. I didn't interrupt anything. Not the police,

EMT'S, the crazies going off on the street, none of that. I walked back in the house, immune to everything. I gave a fuck. Honestly I did.

In this moment though, my mind had went into overdrive, and I didn't know what to do. All I could think about was years ago, when me and him were duckin' inside of Louie's, as a body got dropped right in front of us. I guess God messed up and came back to finish up his original plan. I was now at the back of the house, in the kitchen. No one was in here except me. I slow bopped out of the kitchen, stopping back in the living room, looking out the front door as they finally put cuz's body on a gurney to haul him off to the morgue. The screams were blood curdling, and it was enough to make the hardest of men cry. I walked up the stairs and locked myself in the bathroom. There I balled. And I balled. And I balled. I didn't need this in my life. Not right now. Not ever. What in the good hell did I do to have to live through this? As I drowned in my sorrows, I pulled my phone out of my pocket to see 16 missed calls from my mom. I didn't even go to the voicemail, I just called her straight back.

"Where you at???" I stayed quiet, trying to hide my sniffles as best as possible.

"Lamar what's wrong and where you at?" I gathered myself real quick.

"Edward's dead, ma. He was shot in the car." I cried even more.

"Didn't I tell you that you ain't need to be going anywhere your first night back?" I was beyond heated.

"REALLY MA?? MY DAMN COUSIN IS DEAD AND THE ONLY THING YOU CAN THINK OF TO TELL

ME IS WHY I AIN'T STAY IN THE HOUSE!!!" I didn't even realize I was yelling as loud as I was. **"DON'T WORRY THOUGH!!! I'M GETTING MY STUFF TOMORROW AND LEAVING!!! SHOW HOW MUCH YOU CARE!!!"**

I hung the phone up and just dropped to the floor. If it wasn't one thing it was another. My damn cousin was dead and for my mama to not give condolence but rub it in as to why I didn't stay in the house, was just appalling. I didn't wanna be in that house anymore. I didn't wanna see anyone in this damn city anymore. I just wanted to die to be quite honest.

My mom was once again blowing up my phone, but I could care less. She had pissed me off to the highest level of pistivity. I didn't wanna talk to her, nor anyone else. Just then, there was a knock at the door. I slowly got up and snatched it open out of pure anger. I looked down to see my little two year old cousin MJ. He slept through the whole thing in an upstairs bedroom. Here he was, standing in every ounce of innocence you could imagine. He stared up at me as I stared back at him. Just then, he did something amazing. He grabbed a bunch of toilet paper off the roll. "Here, no cry," he said, as he handed me the bundled up paper. I grabbed it, amazed at his smile and innocence. He then hugged me around my legs and just held on to me. Crazy as this may sound, he made me forget about everything that had just happened, if even for a quick moment. I picked him up and went back into the room. It was late, but he was up. I cut on the television to the Cartoon Network and we proceeded to watch The Flintstones. As I lie there in bed with him curled up under me, I slowly got my sanity back. He was busy laughing at the cartoon, while I was busy coming back around to myself. How can kids do this to us though? It was something about the spark in their eyes that told us to keep going. My lil cuz MJ, that's exactly what he did. My arm stayed wrapped around him until we both fell asleep.

The sun came creepin' through the window in the morning. The door was shut, MJ was gone and the TV was off. My eyes just stayed open, looking around the room, not thinking bout a damn thing. The house was quiet from what I could hear. I got up, sitting on the edge of the bed, distant from the rest of the world. I really didn't wanna leave this room. If I could stay trapped forever, I would have, however, I couldn't. I had to face reality. I walked out the room to the smell of grits. I knew grits when I smelled it. I made it downstairs to the kitchen, where Wanda and Nikki were conversing as Nikki continued to stir the pot.

"Oh you up I see. Gone head and sit down." I looked at Nikki with a WTF look.

"How you so upbeat after last night?"

"Trust, we not, but you need to hear what we bout to tell you." I looked over at Wanda as she just sipped some tea at the table.

"What you lookin at me for? Sit down." Hesitantly, I pulled out a seat and just put my head in my hand. Nikki fixed us all plates of grits and sausage, and brought em all to the table.

"Aight look," Nikki started off as she took a seat. "First off, it's sad. We all sad. Don't pull this shit about we upbeat, cause regardless of what happens, I ain't mopin' around. Now, was it fucked up what happened to cuz? Yes!!! Did he bring it on himself? Yes!!! Yo cousin was in a lot of shit. We were his safe haven. Last night though, his lifestyle finally caught up to him, which leaves me to my last statement. Leave these trife ass bitches alone. You keep playin with fire and someone gone burn yo ass. Now we gotta go kill a bitch!!!" I just sat there, taking slow scoops of my grits.

"You serious Nikki?"

"YES!!!," both her and Wanda said in unison.

"Yo *** damn cousin was fuckin' half of Detroit, and half of Detroit was either trife, married to a nigga, or married to a bitch that looked like a nigga." I just flopped back in my chair. I looked over at Wanda, and she nodded her head in agreement. Damn, I knew cuz was a little bit wild, but I didn't know he had gotten that deep into his shit where he had folks out to kill him. I automatically started to think about 'A Thin Line Between Love and Hate' where Darnell was the man until he met Brandy. Brandy wasn't no easy win, and when he flipped on her, she snapped off. Nobody deserved to have that happen to them, but you reap what you sow.

"Where's Crystal?," I asked.

"One of her friends took her last night. The rest of the fam disappeared as well. Shit wasn't the easiest to deal with," Wanda said. She was right, though. It wasn't, and I had even more demons to face when I got back home to the East Side with my mama. I finished up and went outside to the streets in front of the house. I observed the now ripped caution tape, the blood stains on the ground, shards of glass that didn't get scraped up and one shell casing they missed. I picked it up and stood there, alone, with no one else around. I gazed down the block to the far end of the street. In the distance through my squinted eyes, I could see a wino draggin' himself, moving his hands as if he were having the best conversation on Earth. I turned back to my right and there was a kid on a bike, coming up the cross street. He was in a black hoodie, and we locked eye contact with each other. He slowly cruised by. We looked at each other with the 'who the fuck are you' stare. I followed him down the next street as he slowed down to look back. He flashed some hand sign at me and then sped off, going to do whatever he was going to do. It was deja vu like a muthafucka, and it was eerie as hell. I closed my eyes and took a whiff of the air. It smelled like death. I inhaled it. I had to embrace this for some strange reason. If you are afraid to die, then you are afraid to live, and I damn sure wasn't afraid of either. I opened my eyes to the sight of an old lady across the street, staring dead at me as she rocked back and forth in her patio chair. She waved at me with a Bible in her hand. I didn't do anything back. I just turned around and walked back into the house.

A few hours later around one o'clock, Nikki gave me a ride back to the crib. It was an uneasy feeling, knowing that me and my mama got into it. She hadn't called me all day, which let me know she wasn't very fond of me right now. My pops, he found out about Edward early in the morning from Nikki. He hadn't called me, but he was straight since he knew that I was alright. He was now at work and this house was about to get very uncomfortable. I unlocked the door and opened it very slowly. There was an uneasy silence. She wasn't in the living room. I walked through to look in the kitchen. No one was there either. I walked down to the basement. She wasn't down there either. Where in the hell was she at?

"**MAMA??,**" I yelled out. No response. I continued calling out her name as I went back upstairs. I looked in her bedroom, my bedroom, and nothing. Her car was outside, so where in the world was she at? It didn't even matter anymore. I called for a cab while I started to pack my bags, which wasn't nothing but putting my toiletries in there. It would be about 25 minutes until the cab got there. This was strange. I didn't know where my mom was. I luckily managed to get a seven o'clock flight out. It was a hell of a hefty price to get a last minute joint back to Vegas, but it was worth it to roll up out of here.

As I waited, I debated on calling my moms. One dispute did not destroy my love for her, but I knew there was a rift between us. I had to apologize in some form, shape or way. My cousin just died and I didn't want to hold in any animosity towards the woman who birthed me and raised me because it would be messed up if something happened to her and I didn't have the chance to make amends. Forgiveness was so key for me, especially seeing that my lack of forgiveness was a part of the reason that I was a disengaged man instead of a married one. Yea, both sides played a part like I said, but holding on to some shit I should've let go of took it's toll, and it's only so much apologizing one person is gonna do. I was in between a rock and a hard place. I didn't wanna risk an argument. Finally, I went over to the computer in the living room. I pulled out some paper from the printer and wrote a short few lines explaining everything.

MA,

    I WAS WRONG. I NEVER MEANT TO UPSET OR DISRESPECT YOU. PLEASE FIND IT IN YOUR HEART TO FORGIVE ME. I WILL TEXT YOU WHEN I ARRIVE IN VEGAS. I HOPE WE CAN PUT THIS BEHIND US BOTH. LOVE YOUR SON.

It was short and nothing extraordinary, but it did get straight to the point like she always did. I hoped this would make amends. I folded it up and left it inside of her puzzle book in the kitchen where I knew she would find it. I walked back to the front door, looking out into the street on my lowly block. This had to be the quickest coming and going visit in the history of man. I just couldn't stay though. This life wasn't for me anymore. Not this life. Not these surroundings. I know every place had a ghetto, but here it was a lil crazier than the norm. Combine that with death and uneasiness occurring within my own family, and I honestly didn't know if I ever wanted to come back here ever again. Plus, I would probably be hated by my whole family for leaving before Eddie's funeral.

The cabby pulled up. As I got my bags and headed out the door, I seen my dad's truck pull up in the driveway. It shocked me 'cause I thought he was at work. My mom was in the passenger seat. I took a deep breath and went down to the bottom of the steps, signaling to the cab driver to give me a quick minute.

"Mom?," I said as she exited the truck and walked towards the door. "Mom?" She walked right past me, not saying anything, nor looking at me. My dad, however, came up and put his hand on my shoulder.

"Ahh, she'll be okay boy. See you when you get back." It was nothing to him. I was a grown man like he always said. He never questioned my decisions. He just let me do me.

"Later Daddy!!!"

"Yep," he yelled back as he proceeded into the house, not even looking back. I just felt terrible. I slow bopped to the cab, put my bags in, and I was on my way to the airport in my home city, probably for the last time.

I got into Vegas a lil bit after 9:00 p.m. Pacific time. I didn't tell anyone that I was returning. I got my bags and paid for a cab ride straight to the crib. Yea, I had spent unnecessary money that I didn't have too, but I really didn't care. I just wanted to be left alone. The drive back to the house felt more like a drive to a prison where I would be held in solitary confinement. I had no one special to lean on. Those days were gone. I could call family, but it wouldn't feel the same as having comfort from a woman you loved. It ain't bad being single, it's just bad when you know you fucked something good up. I got to my place that night with plans on just watching TV until it started watching me. I checked the mailbox real quick and seen I had a package. What it was, I had no clue. I walked into my dark two bedroom apartment and just plopped on the couch. I sat there in the dark, wondering was I gonna be like this for the next two weeks. I can't front. I was depressed.

No fiancee, family rifts, unforeseen circumstances that were coming. I wasn't myself. Hell, I started to question whether or not was I even worthy of taking on such a new challenge. Was I even worthy of living this life anymore? I knew I shouldn't be feeling like this. There were people in way worse situations than me. People were homeless. People were going through divorces with kids that were confused. People were just going through way more difficult shit than I ever was. I sat and I sat and I sat. I sat until I looked up and realized it was 11:17. *Shit,* I thought. I just wasted almost two hours of my life feeling sorry for myself. I couldn't keep doing this.

I walked to my bathroom and got showered up. As I finished up and began to start shaving, I stopped. I gazed into the mirror. I looked at myself. It felt like there was two of me and the nigga on the other side was looking at me like "you ain't bout that life." I closed my eyes, opened 'em back up and I swear I seen the devil. I jumped back, scared as shit. I didn't know what to make of what just happened. I took a minute to walk out on my patio to catch myself. My breathing was deep and my heart was pounding like John Henry on the train tracks. And then it hit me. John Henry, the mythical black man who hammered through a mountain faster than a huge drill. They thought he couldn't do it, but he did. I didn't feel better, but for a split second, I felt that I could accomplish much once again, even with the circumstances being how they were. I walked back in the bathroom, trimming and lining the goatee up. The obvious would be to head to bed after this, but I was nowhere near tired. I was wired off of pure adrenaline from the last 48 hours. I cut the TV on in my bedroom and flipped through the channels as usual. Nothing was on that caught my attention. It was the usual late night shenanigans of TV.

Lame ass infomercials. Just when I was about to say fuck it, I became perplexed. I came across VH1 Soul. An oldie, but goodie was on that got me vibin'. R. Kelly's 'I Believe I Can Fly' was just coming on. It was amazing that a man known for pissing on folks had a song that just captivated the spirit of every individual on Earth when they were in doubt. I sat there and delved deep into that video, taking in every word. Someone or some unknown force was telling me something. Whether it was God, a deceased family member or just a damn coincidence, I was having a message delivered to me. After that video finished, I turned over and slept the night away.

4 THE STORM

Time flew by faster than Dale Earnhardt, Jr. at a NASCAR race track. It was May 8th, the day before I was supposed to fly out. The head honchos at my occupation had taken care of everything as far as me being settled in over there. They shipped my car, my furniture, and got me in a condo over there with a bomb ass view from the pics I had seen. I didn't try to get too excited, seeing how advertisements could fool the hell out of you sometimes. I was ready though. I had two months to prepare for this so, if I wasn't ready by now, then I would never be.

My aunt and uncle had let me hold the house down. They were on vacation back East to visit Barry's side of the family so they trusted me to take care of things while they were gone. I started off this morning early. After a good run, which seen me rise up at four in the morning, I began to operate on the stove. This was my last time having breakfast in the states so I had to make it a bomb one. Scrambled eggs with cheese, grits, applewood bacon, biscuits and some leftover ham. Yea, a brother had two different forms of swine on the plate. It was 6:02 in the morning now and I was feeling like a million bucks. I had the house all to myself and I was gravy. All my worries and cares were gone. Me and my mom, we hadn't talked since I left the crib. I reached out to her, but she never accepted my calls. I stopped worrying about it. I learned in life that you can't control other people's feelings. All you can do is control your own. I kicked back over this bomb plate of food while watching the early morning news. It was basically the same as every major city. People disagreeing with city officials. The investigative reporter found out DMV workers were hooking their friends up with licenses without proper credentials. Someone was robbed, shot, murdered, in a car accident, and one crazy white person was caught running up Sahara ass naked. Hey, it was Las Vegas so that wasn't a surprise at all.

I was chillin' something serious, until something clicked in my head. The day I got back from Detroit, I received a package in the mail. I never opened it. I did however place it in my luggage that I was taking with me. I shot up over to the room, searching through the mounds and mounds of clothes until I found it. I picked up this small package, not knowing what the hell was in it. I shook it up, but I heard nothing moving around. I looked at the sender's address. It was from a watch store in Guam. I didn't know anyone over there. Hey, maybe someone was sending me a welcome to the Island gift. I opened the box up and discovered a sleek, chrome Burberry case. I opened it up and was amazed at what I seen. This shit was cleaner than a baby ass cleaned out with a garden hose. A leather Burberry pattern band with a chrome outer face and black face inside. The shit was crazy. As I soaked in the sheer quality of this timepiece, I found a card inside. I turned it over and read it.

"Welcome to the Island. I look forward to G moves. I will pick you up from the airport. HAFA ADAI." I ain't know what the hell a hafa adai meant, but it had to be something good since the message was gravy. My mouth formed up into a smile. I thought I was going over there all alone, not knowing a soul. It was obvious that somebody knew me or knew of me. Judging from the note, we were about to have some serious encounters when I got up over there. It was kind of cool, yet kind of creepy at the same time. Oh boy, this was something else I could add to the list of crazy life experiences. I put everything back in the box and stuffed it down in my suitcase. I went back over to finish my now semi warm breakfast, set my alarm for 9 a.m. and proceeded to get a rejuvenating nap in. It didn't last long, as about 45 minutes into my snore session, my phone got to buzzin. It was Tony with an elongated paragraph in which he pretty much told me good luck on my new journey tomorrow. I mean the nigga could've just said good luck, but you know some cats get sentimental.

I looked at the time on my phone, 7:17. I was tired as hell, but I couldn't go back to sleep fully. I slept in spurts which seemed like forever. When I would wake up though, only three to five minutes would pass. I just began to lie there with my eyes wide open. The fan was on blast, my whole body was under the covers and reality started to sink in. In about 24 hours, my flight would be leaving from Las Vegas to LA, to Tokyo, to Guam. That was a lot of flying, a lot of miles and a lot of faces that I would have to deal with. Most people would spend their last day anywhere probably cutting loose and acting the fool. Me, nah. I would soak in every inch of this house and let it be my last memory. Finally, after kickin' the lazy bug up off me, I got up and walked into my Aunt's room. There, I looked at old pics she had hanging. My grandmother, my aunt when she was younger, cousins and others I completely did not know. Then I came across one of me and my cousin, which was her daughter at her old house back in the D. Flashbacks occurred as a smile draped across my face. Way before Vegas and way before she met the man of her dreams, my aunt's house in the D was my escape. Spending the night over there gave me a break from the turmoil going on at my parent's house. Over there, things were simple. I played Super Nintendo in her basement, watched TV and indulged in bowl after bowl of cereal. She didn't cook shit on the weekends, but if you were hungry, you were guaranteed some cereal. Mainly Cap'n Crunch, because she kept that on deck more than ever. I wish I could go back to those days sometimes. Not particularly my situation, but just being a kid. That's when life wasn't full of bills, responsibility and the constant bullshit of the real world that you had to deal with.

I proceeded over to the outside of her closet where her bookshelf was. I never was an avid reader, but I started to scavenge through the titles to see if anything caught my eye. 'Let Me Pimp or Let Me Die.' 'Family Honor.' 'Fresh Out.' There were some interesting titles to say the least. I kept scanning and scanning until I caught a title that was out of the ordinary. 'BANDAGES.' It was interesting to say the least, because what I took from it was that it was a story about healing. I didn't even pay attention to who the author was, nor did I care. I was just hoping to see a passage or excerpt that caught my eye and would make me think. I flipped open the book to a random page and let my eyes commence to taking a journey.

.........My whole family was gone. Either they were dead or in jail. Aah fuck, this shit hurt. I was fucked up on the inside. This drink wasn't doing anything but killing me even more, but it felt like a friend right now. How could this be happening to me? I thought my grief was over. Of course, though, it only suited me right that bad news come back around. I was tired and felt that I had nothing left to give this world. I grabbed my car keys, drunk and all. 11:20 was the time. I shouldn't have gotten my drunk ass on the road, but I was beyond out of my right mind. I somehow managed to swerve my black ass to the 5 freeway and head South. I was drunk, but I still had some sense of what was around me. The freeway was eerily empty. It was a Friday night and I only seen one other whip on the road with me. Nothing was in my rear view either. It was like someone was telling me it's time. I had no music on or anything. It was just me and my thoughts at this time. I was tired, and I didn't need anymore pain. It was time to end it all. I made it to the Palm Ave. exit headed towards Imperial Beach. Again, I was at the light and it was just me. No other cars or anything. Either the whole world had died, or somebody was seriously fuckin' with me. I made that right and caught all damn greens. This shit was getting more strange by the minute. I booked a hard left down whatever the hell street until I got my ass to the strip where the boardwalk

was. There were literally no cars on the street as I double parked in my drunken mind state. I got out stumbling, groggy and feeling at the lowest of lows.

It was August, but the night was beyond breezy. It felt more like a November night out here. I stumbled slowly over to the beginning of the pier. I looked at the pretty lights of the boardwalk sign. The red and yellow. It kind of looked like a bootleg ass golden arch. I stood there and gazed at it for a minute until all of a sudden, the lights went out. The shit got even stranger now. I focused my eyes as much as I could down the pier. There wasn't a soul in sight. The only other life I seen were two pelicans. I slowly started my drunken descent towards the middle of The Boardwalk. I had nothing else to live for. Everyone was out of my life and I had no other reason to continue on. I got to the middle of the pier and walked over to the side, leaning against the old wooden sides as I watched and listened to the waves crash. The moonlight gave it an eerie glow. I began to cry as I looked up at the star lit sky. "Mama, I failed. It's time." I reached in my back pocket, grabbing the little notepad that I always kept on me. I pulled out a pen and wrote my final thoughts for the world on there.

"TO THE ONE WHO MAY READ THIS, KNOW I LEAVE THIS EARTH UNFULFILLED, KNOW THE THRILL OF LIFE WAS A ROLLER COASTER THAT GOT STUCK AT THE TOP, SO I TOOK THE PLUNGE, RATHER JUMPING TO SEE HOW THE GROUND FEELS, INSTEAD OF WAITING FOR SOMEONE TO RESCUE ME, BECAUSE FOR THEM TO SAVE ME, MEANS THEY WILL TAKE ON MY BURDENS, SEE I'VE BEEN HURTING FOR TOO LONG, STRONG IS WHAT THEY TELL ME TO BE, BUT WEAK LINKS IN MY DNA

BROKE THE CHAIN, AND I AM SIMPLY......A LIFE NOT WORTH LIVING."

*I tossed that green notepad to the middle of the pier. This was it. "GOODBYE WORLD!!!," I yelled, hoping that someone would hear my last cry and be witness to my last hoorah upon this Earth. I placed both feet on the middle beam and got my balance. I simply closed my eyes and outstretched my arms as if I were Jesus Christ himself. This was it. 10...hitting Richard with that rock flashed in my mind. 9...helping rob a man flashed. 8...Sitting in a prison cell flashed. 7...Boot camp flashed. 6...Landing in Bahrain flashed. 5...Talking to Star for the first time in Hawaii flashed. 4...Making love to Star for the first time flashed. 3...Getting slammed face first on the hood of a police car flashed. 2....Loving life on the ocean flashed. 1.......Carl Lamell Jackson flashed. I flashed in my own mind as I leaned and fell. **THUMP!!!** My head hit the hard, cold surface.*

I read that and shut the book with authority. That was intense as hell. I didn't know the prelude or anything else that had led up to that young brother doing what he did, but it reminded me of me the day after I came back from the D. *Holy shit,* I thought. It was like someone had a camera on my life and recorded what I would have probably done if I didn't get my thoughts together on that crazy night. I sat down on auntie's bed and just caught myself for a moment. I was really trying to soak in what I just read. Carl Lamell Jackson sounded a lot similar to Lamar Atteley III. I went back to my room, turned off the alarm on my phone and closed my eyes. I would definitely sleep now because I was literally scared shitless by the irony of what I had just read. When I arose, it was two o'clock on the dot. That meant I had exactly 17 hours before I was to take off on a journey over the Pacific. *Fuck this,* I thought. I wasn't gonna stay couped up in this house for my last night in the states. I had to at least go out for a drive or something. I texted Jay Hall asking where he was. As usual, he said in the gym. We arranged to meet up later at Protein House. The least I could do with the last of my time was treat this brother to a meal. Even after he became an IFBB pro, he never changed, nor got too big for his own self. A lot of people do exactly the opposite. They hit a little success or get a little bit of fame, and all of a sudden, they are bigger than the entire world. Not my guy. That's what you call a real homey, a real friend.

I still had plenty of time to spare, seeing that we weren't meeting up until seven. I threw on some shorts and a t-shirt and headed down the street to the liquor store for a quick drink and some skins. I didn't know if they would have that fried swine out there in Guam so I had to get my fix while I was still here. I walked in nonchalantly, not worrying about anything. It was your typical afternoon. I was the only one in here. It didn't surprise me, cause who in the hell would wanna drink liquor in the hot ass Vegas afternoon heat? The Arab behind the counter was watching some TV show. Everything was quiet. I grabbed my skins and went towards the freezer. I knew damn well I wasn't gonna get any drank, but it was appealing to look at. I needed to quit trippin though. I knew they would have alcohol overseas. I just didn't wanna detach myself from the states just yet. I moved a couple of freezer doors down and got me an Arizona Green Tea. This was my feel good drink, and I strolled to the counter with that feel good walk.

"Hello," said the clerk with that usual Arabic accent.

"Sup man. Here's $2.50. Keep the change."

"Thank you my friend." I took three steps towards the door.

"NIGGA, GET YO BITCH ASS BACK!!!" All I seen was a shotgun barrel in my face. I dropped everything. The nigga pushed me to the ground.

"YOU WANNA LIVE THEN SHUT YO ASS UP!!!" I stared at him and this barrel. My heart was pounding, my hands were down by my side and the look in this dudes eyes through that ski mask was saying try me.

"HURRY UP ABU DHABI!!!" I heard the other dude screaming at the cashier for the money.

"Tell me one reason I shouldn't blow yo head off right now?" Dude asked me a question that I really didn't have an answer that he wanted to hear. Yea, I could easily say cause I wanna live and get fucked up from several rounds. So, I thought to myself, here goes nothing.

"Because I'm headed overseas to work with service niggas." His look got a lil different. The gun was still in my face, but I can tell I struck a chord with him.

"Yea, G shit nigga. Semper Fi, even though they kicked me out."

POP!! POP!! Two gunshots went off and them niggas booked it. As they ran out the door, ol boy who was locked and loaded on my ass screamed out

"PROTECT YO'SELF MY NIGGA!!!" and booked it. I jumped up after about five seconds to see blood splattered along the wall and the counter. They smoked his ass and I wasn't staying around to see what was gonna happen. I high tailed it out of there with no snack or tea in hand. I got straight in the car and peeled the fuck out. Great, I thought.

This was just what I needed on my last day here. I witnessed a murder and almost got my life taken as well.

The ride less than half a mile down the road seemed like a 400 mile journey from Vegas to wherever. Everything seemed to be going in slow motion. I know by now somebody had went in and discovered ol' boy's bloody corpse. Pretty sure there were cameras in there, so I knew the cops would see that I didn't do nothing but take off when the coast was clear. I got back to my aunt's crib and hustled inside. I went to the kitchen to pour me a glass of almond milk and came back to sit on the couch. The way I was drinking this you would've swore it was an alcoholic beverage. I was shaking, nervous, distraught, all the above. This was too much trauma to deal with in the time span of just one month. It was like God gave me good news and then He said, "HA NIGGA!!!" I knew it wasn't the case, but it's crazy what goes through your head when you're down and out. My face fell to my palms. What the hell was next I thought? That's when my phone rang.

Me: "Jay, what's good?"

Jay: "A man, something wrong with Justin. I'm on my way to the vet right now. So.......I won't make it to eat. However, whoop ass over there since I won't see you. I gotta make sure my son straight, aight?"

Me: "Aight bro. Hope all is well with him. Be easy mane and I'll see you whenever mane."

Jay: "Yep. Later Butler!!!"

Me" "Gone."

I fucking jinxed myself. That was the icing on a fucked up cake made out of pure shit. Yea, it sounded nasty and crazy, but this was too much to deal with. I didn't wanna go anywhere, didn't wanna see anyone, none of that. Hell, I ain't even wanna be in this position right now. It sucked like hell. My world had officially crashed in and I felt like I was floating in space. I hadn't felt like this since I left my daughter in Texas and it was sad cause I could never see her ever again. I swear, sometimes, even when a man handles business, he is still looked upon as the enemy. I looked up at the clock. It was 4:01. I decided at that moment that it would be a night of being alone by myself, stuck in my own world. I cut my phone off. I wanted no disturbances. If one of my boys were hangin' off a cliff and needed me, well they were gonna be shit out of luck today. I cut on the TV. Lo and behold, Martin was on. From clicking guide on the remote, I see episodes were coming on straight til 10:00. I just sat there, hoping laughter could indeed become the best medicine for me. Two hours in though, it was like my medicine was a bootleg potion made in the back of a barn. I didn't laugh for shit. Even when looking at my favorite episode, where Shanana had to take a grinder to Myra's toes. Even that couldn't get me to laugh.

Now it was after six. This wasn't working. I flipped through the channels until I landed on Comedy Central. My favorite movie 'Coming To America' was on. I just knew this would make me feel better, especially seeing how on cable they altered the curse words with some stupid voice over. An hour into the movie though, it was the same exact result. No laughter at all. I couldn't believe this at all. It was now 7:13, and my last night was turning out to be the worst night of my life.

I cut the TV off and walked out to the backyard. It was peaceful out here, and peace was something that I definitely needed right now. The breeze that was coming off the mountains was perfect. The sun's glaring light was fading out slowly. There were a rare flock of birds that were flying out to wherever. The sounds of cars passing by also added an eerie, yet settling feeling to me. This was it for the stateside life. Tomorrow at 9:00 a.m. it would be all over. I soaked in the sights and didn't think much of anything else. I walked back in the house and into the kitchen. I pulled out four eggs, some shredded cheese and some grits. This would be my last meal. I took this moment as if I were residing on Death Row and this was the last big hoorah for me. My death would come the minute I stepped foot on the plane. This food here would be me passing the torch to myself. I was determined to redefine myself and find my purpose in life. I stirred those grits a little bit slower that night. I saw my life in them. The more I stirred, the looser they got. That's how I wanted to feel. My life was tough at this moment. Over time, I wanted it to loosen up and get easier. I poured the right amount of salt in there and added about a half stick of butter. There would be no sugar in my grits. That shit was nasty and anybody who said that sugar in your grits is good, is a damn nutcase. I tried that mess one time and damn near threw up.

I put my grits on low heat and proceeded to crack those eggs in a bowl and whip em up. I poured a little bit of almond milk up in 'em to add some extra flare to it. Fuck it,

I thought. Why not go all the way in with my last dinner. I grabbed some chopped bacon seasoning out the cabinet, mixing it in for that swine flavor. I went back to the fridge, found me some chopped up mushrooms and got em ready for destruction. The skillet was just about heated right. I poured those mushrooms in there and closed my eyes, inhaling the aroma from them 'shrooms. Who in the hell would ever think a simple meal could mean so much? I let em saute for a minute, then added the eggs. I thought how amazing it was that food was clearing my mind. I added the cheese and finished up my stove top masterpiece.

I fixed my plate and headed back over to the couch to indulge. I flipped the TV as usual, expecting to find the usual crazy sitcoms. I got to HBO, and again, I ran across Def Jam Poetry. It seems like every time I was bored, this was on. I sat there and watched it for whatever reason I don't even know. Just as I was gonna turn the channel, one of the best soulful singers of all time came on the stage. Smokey Robinson was indeed a legend. Not only because of his vocals to me, but he was also from my hometown of Detroit. I had to give respect to anyone who made it from the crib and was doing great things. I decided to hit the DVR recorder on the TV and listen to what this man had to spit. He started to go in with a piece he titled 'A Black American.'

"I love being Black. I love being called Black. I love being an American.
I love being a Black American, but as a Black man in this country I think it's a shame
That every few years we get a change of name.

Since those first ships arrived here from Africa that came
across the sea
There were already Black men in this country who were
free.
And as for those that came over here on those terrible
boats,
They were called nigga and slave
And told what to do and how to behave.

And then master started trippin' and doing his midnight
tippin',
Down to the slave shacks where he forced he and Great-
Great Grandma to be together,
And if Great-Great Grandpa protested, he got tarred and
feathered.

And at the same time, the Black men in the country who
were free,
Were mating with the tribes like the Apache and the
Cherokee.
And as a result of all that, we're a parade of every shade.
And as in this late day and age, you can be sure,
They ain't too many of us in this country whose
bloodline is pure.

But, according to a geological, geographical, genealogy
study published in Time Magazine,
The Black African people were the first on the scene,
So for what it's worth, the Black African people were the
first on earth

And through migration, our characteristics started to
change, and rearrange,
To adapt to whatever climate we migrated to.
And that's how I became me and you became you.

So, if we gonna go back, let's go all the way back,
And if Adam was Black and Eve was Black,
Then that kind of makes it a natural fact that everybody
in America is an African American.

Everybody in Europe is an African European; everybody
in the Orient is an African Asian
And so on and so on,
That is, if the origin of man is what we're gonna go on.
And if one drop of Black blood makes you Black like they
say,
Then everybody's Black anyway.

So quit trying to change my identity.
I'm already who I was meant to be
I'm a Black American, born and raised.
And brother James Brown wrote a wonderful phrase,
"Say it loud, I'm Black and I'm proud! Say it loud, I'm
Black and I'm proud!"

Cause I'm proud to be Black and I ain't never lived in
Africa,
And 'cause my Great-Great Granddaddy on my Daddy's
side did, don't mean I want to go back.
Now I have nothing against Africa,

It's where some of the most beautiful places and people in
the world are found.
But I've been blessed to go a lot of places in this world,
And if you ask me where I choose to live, I pick America,
hands down.

Now, by and by, we were called Negroes, and after while,
that name has vanished.
Anyway, Negro is just how you say "black" in Spanish.
Then, we were called colored, but ****, everybody's one
color or another,
And I think it's a shame that we hold that against each
other.

And it seems like we reverted back to a time when being
called Black was an insult,
Even if it was another Black man who said it, a fight
would result,
Cause we've been so brainwashed that Black was wrong,
So that even the yellow niggas and black niggas couldn't
get along.

But then, came the 1960s; when we struggled and died to
be called equal and Black,
And we walked with pride with our heads held high and
our shoulders pushed back,
And Black was beautiful.

But, I guess that wasn't good enough,
Cause now here they come with some other stuff.
Who comes up with this **** anyway?

Was it one, or a group of niggahs sitting around one day?

Feelin' a little insecure again about being called Black
And decided that African American sounded a little more
exotic.
Well, I think you were being a little more neurotic.

It's that same mentality that got "Amos and Andy" put
off the air,
Cause' they were embarrassed about the way the
character's spoke.
And as a result of that action, a lot of wonderful Black
actors ended up broke.
When we were just laughin' and have fun about
ourselves.
So I say, "**** you if you can't take a joke."
You didn't see the Beverly Hillbilly's being protested by
white folks.

And if you think, that cause you think that being called
African American set all Black people's mind at ease.....

Since we affectionately call each other "nigga",

I affectionately say to you, "nigga Please".

How come I didn't get the chance to vote on who I'd like
to be?
Who gave you the right to make that decision for me?
I ain't under your rule or in your dominion
And I am entitled to my own opinion.

Joe McClain Jr.

Now there are some African Americans here,
But they recently moved here from places like Kenya,
Ethiopia, Zambia, Zimbabwe, and Zaire.
But, now the brother who's family has lived in the
country for generations,
Occupying space in all the locations
New York, Miami, L.A., Detroit, Chicago-
Even if he's wearing a dashiki and sporting an afro.

And, if you go to Africa in search of your race,
You'll find out quick you're not an African American,
You're just a Black American in Africa takin' up space.

Why you keep trying to attach yourself to a continent,
Where if you got the chance and you went,
Most people there wouldn't even claim you as one of
them; as a pure bred daughter or son of them.
Your heritage is right here now, no matter what you call
yourself or what you say
And a lot of people died to make it that way.
And if you think America is a leader on inequality and
suffering and grievin'
How come there so many people comin' and so few
leavin'?

Rather than all this 'find fault with America' **** you
promotin',
If you want to change something, use your privilege, get
to the polls!
Commence to votin'!

God knows we've earned the right to be called American
Americans and be free at last.
And rather than you movin' forward progress, you
dwelling in the past.
We've struggled too long; we've come too far.
Instead of focusing on who we were, let's be proud of
who we are.

We are the only people whose name is always a trend.
When is this **** gonna end?
Look at all the different colors of our skin-
Black is not our color. It's our core.
It's what we been livin' and fightin' and dyin' for.

But if you choose to be called African American and
that's your preference
Then I 'll give you that reference

But I know on this issue I don't stand alone on my own
and if I do, then let me be me
And I'd appreciate it if when you see me, you'd say,
"there goes a man who says it loud I'm Black. I'm Black. I'm
a Black American, and I'm proud

Cause I love being an American. And I love being Black. I
love being called Black.

Yeah, I said it, and I don't take it back."

As the audience applauded, I took a moment to mute the TV. I was in stunned silence. This man just went in on some real G shit. I Had never been a fan of poetry ever before in my life. In a mere six minutes, my whole philosophy on the art of poetry changed. I finished off the rest of my grits and scrambled around the house to find a pen and a piece of paper. Fuck washing this dish, I thought. If the food stuck to the plate forever, I could careless. Finally, I looked in my aunt's closet and found exactly what I was looking for. A solo notebook with a gang of pens. It was probably something she ain't even know she had. I ran back to the living room and flipped through it. There were no notes, no anything written down. Cool beans, I thought. Here was my chance to profile a new side of myself to not only myself, but to the world. I took a deep breath, and just began to write.

REGRET

Payback minded
unwilling to forgive
rather live being the asshole
than to accept genuine apologies
becoming something you are not
flip flopping between your feelings
no longer giving a damn

because the world says man is not

supposed to

tossing away life

tossing away everything

not realizing the value of everything

until you are left with nothing

and at that moment

regret kicks in and you sit and ponder

what if

but if the word if was a fifth

it would be drunk already

I looked at the time. It was 8:29. I wrote that time in the corner of the paper as a reminder to myself to when I completed my first poem. I read it over and over about six or seven times. I really didn't comprehend what I had just wrote. Deep down, I didn't even know what it meant. It just sounded good as I was writing. I kept staring at it in disbelief. *I really just did this*, I thought. I got up, walked to the room and placed it in my suitcase. This was gonna come in handy in the future, I thought. I didn't know for what, but I just knew it would. I went back to wash my plate off, which was probably permanently bonded with grits residue by now. I handled that, took a shower and literally took one huge leap into the bed. The clock read 9:37. This would be my last memory before I closed my eyes. Tomorrow, when the airport driver came to pick me up at six in the morning, it would be on. I told myself good night and crashed out with a prayer to Jesus for the ages.

"Dear God, in two years, make me not realize who I am today. Amen."

Too many, that isn't a prayer that takes their breath away. However, for me, it was the biggest and baddest prayer that I ever uttered off of my lips, seeing that prayer wasn't one of my strongest suits. I closed my eyes and looked forward to 5 o'clock in the morning.

The alarm started going off faster than I had expected. It had seemed like I had just went to sleep. I mean, I slept good, don't get me wrong. I just wish it would have lasted a little bit longer. I stayed there, staring into the darkness for a good five minutes. The time was here and the time was now. After brushing my teeth and throwing on my clothes, I sat patiently at the door, waiting for the driver to show up. Placing my aunt's keys on the table, I came to the realization that this was the last American house I would leave out of for a long time. The driver pulled up to the house. I took a deep breath and grabbed my two bags. I turned back for one last look.

"I LEAVE BROKEN. I COME BACK RENEWED!!!" I shouted that shit out loud. For what reason? I had no idea. I guess I was just hoping the success spirits of the world would hear me and remember my words. I walked out the door and into my new life. Time flew by quickly. As soon as it seemed that I left the house, I was in seat 49C, getting ready for a quick trip to LAX. I pulled out my laptop to just write. I figured ever since I wrote that poem, I would just keep writing to see if I could create more masterpieces. At least in my head they were masterpieces. We took off and were in the air. I cranked up some Soope da RoadRunner. The 'Where in The World is Soope' mixtape hosted by DJ Skee to be exact. He was an artist out of Gary, Indiana. Brother was hot in the streets and he had that perfect vibin' music that I needed right now. By the time I started to really get into the meat of the music though, it was time to put my shit up. We were descending into Los Angeles. I didn't have any time to mess around, though. I had 30 minutes between when I landed and my next flight out to Japan, which would be 12 hours. How in the good hell was I gonna survive in the air that long? I had no idea. I just knew that I didn't have a choice.

We finally dropped down to LA and exited the plane. Lucky for me, my terminal to Japan was only two terminals down from where I got out, so that was gravy. I checked in and got directed to head to the pre board area. I guess working for the government had its perks, seeing that I would be one of the first ones to get on the bus to drive over to a massive Boeing 777. From the looks of it, I was the only brother on this flight. I didn't feel nervous, seeing that I was almost the tallest brother on the flight it looked like. We loaded up on the first bus and took a slow, yet short drive over to the plane. Man this bitch looked like something from outer space. From the looks of the plane and the amount of people in the airport, I could make a rough guestimate that it would be at least 400 people on this flight.

I waltzed on this plane and it was like stepping into a whole new world. Six seats in each row, including seven throughout the middle rows. This was some crazy off the wall shit. This was nothing that I could've ever imagined. As the plane started to fill up, I started to realize that if these Japanese people wanted to get revenge on me for what the U.S. did to them in World War 2, this would be the perfect time. I quickly nixed my mind of that thought as they started to announce the instructions in both English and Japanese.

"This flight will be approximately 11 hours and 41 minutes." That's all I took away from it. That was gonna be a long time flying over water. I was okay flying over land. Over water though? Hell to the nah!!! Man, all those old planes that I always heard about falling in the water was not cool at this moment. At least if I fell over land, folks could locate my body real fast and get me sent home to be fly in my casket. If I crashed in the ocean, my body might never be found. Worse than that, I might survive the crash, but end up getting ate by a shark, a whale or some giant squid whose arms looked like some bad extensions on some hoodrat project chick's head. Right then, I just lowered my head and started to repeat,

"Please God don't let me die." I said that over and over about a thousand times. "

Are you straight mane?" I looked up to see it was a brother next to me. I didn't even notice he had sat next to me, seeing that I was so zoned out.

"Yea man I'm good. You visiting Tokyo?"

"Naw mane. I'm moving to Guam. I'm in the service and getting stationed out there. Puncho." He extended his hand out and I returned the gratitude.

"Lamar. I'm headed there, too. Taking a Civi job on the Air Force base." His eyes lit up.

"You gotta girl my nigga?" I wondered why he asked that. Deep down, I was hoping he wasn't no down low nigga.

"Naw mane, why?"

"Look mane," as he dropped the shades from his face. "I'm bout partying, yet at the same time, I'm bout handling my business. You seem like the type of brother who is into both. I tell you what. I'm gone be on the Frank Cable ship out there. Let's exchange e-mails later when we touch down and make things happen." I nodded my head in agreeance.

"I'm with it playa." We gave each other a fist pound and continued to chop it up as we took off on this long to death flight. By the time we finished our convo and threw on the headphones, one hour and six minutes had elapsed. Damn, I was totally immune to even being in the air. This was cool though, knowing that I had at least one connect when I got here. Well, technically two, whoever the person was that said they were gonna see me at the airport. I searched the screen on the back of my seat. I ain't feel like watching a movie so I let music become my best friend. I found Wale's 'Ambition' album and let it have a relationship with my ears. The zone out was on as 'Miami Nights' started to crank. Slowly, but surely, the music started to fade away as I faded into dreamworld. I was probably slobbering all over myself. By the time I came to, I seen that over four hours had elapsed on this flight. I missed the lunch meal, but luckily a stewardess was walking by right when I woke up. She asked me was I hungry and I implied, "greatly." I received some cheese pizza and mixed vegetables. It was an odd combination, but one that was filling none the less.

As I smashed, I observed that half of this plane was knocked out. Puncho included. There was an eerie silence minus the obvious plane noise. The flight was smooth and I was soaking it in. I clicked through the option menu on the

TV once again where I ended up picking Paranormal Activity 2. Why did I pick this rat ass of a movie? I really didn't know. Hell, the first one was complete and utter garbage to me. I guess I figured I could give it another go around. After almost two hours, I finally realized that those were two hours that I could not get back in my life. That movie was more trash than the first one.

Since that was over and I still had over five hours left on this plane, it was Hangover 3 time. I hadn't seen it yet, but I heard it was pretty funny. They were right. I tried to hold my laughter in as much as possible, seeing that there were still others around me who were sleep, but that shit wasn't happening. This damn movie tickled my funny bone. Unlike watching Martin before I left the crib, this was actually doing its job. What a way to enjoy myself I thought. However, the butterflies were creepin' into my stomach more and more. It still seemed like a long while away, but I knew soon we would be touching down in Japan. I would only have a few more hours to go until my new life began. *Oh man, what a life it would be,* I thought.

"Welcome to Tokyo." I didn't understand anything they were saying in Japanese, but I comprehended that. Ahh man, it was a reality.

"A boss, you got a layover?," Puncho asked me.

"Yea bruh, I got two hours to chill before I'm up outta here."

"Aight bruh, mine's only 45 minutes, so I'll see you when I see you." We dapped it up and he gave me a business card with his e-mail on it, telling me to hit him up after I get settled down in Guam.

As he took off for his gate, I stalled for a minute. Everything slowed down around me. This was real. I was on the other side of the world. This was some shit that I could only dream of. I had to walk down thru another baggage claim to enter my next terminal. The walk seemed like forever, seeing how this airport was the size of outer space. I made it through baggage claim real quick. Over here, you didn't have to take off your shoes, so that made things a whole lot quicker and easier. Finally, after God knows how long, I got to my terminal. It was about six people over here. There were probably more coming, but I hoped not. I wanted to be spaced out on my flight, seeing that I had been couped up for 12 hours.

I didn't exchange any money on the way over here, so I didn't have a chance to indulge in any Japanese cuisine of the nearby restaurants. I just patiently waited and waited like a loner. Things were quiet over here. About twenty more people made it to the terminal and that was it. I looked up at the clock to see it read 8:14. No sooner than I did that, the announcement came that we were about to begin boarding for the four hour flight from here to Guam. My heart started beating faster than a man who ain't had no ass in six months and was scared of bustin' quick the minute he got some.

The thump of the wheels touching the ground were equivalent to a bomb going off. At least that's how I felt in my mind. I was here finally. 12:49 a.m. on May 10, 2012. I don't know what time it was back in Vegas, but I knew this was more than a major shift. Seeing that I was the only one in my row, I did myself a favor and allowed all of the other passengers to depart the plane first. I needed as much time as I could to prepare myself for the unknown. As the last old

Japanese lady moved ever so slow towards the exit, I finally got up, ready to face this challenge head on. I exited off to a stewardess saying "Hafa Adai." It was pronounced Hoffa Day, and I didn't know what in the hell it really meant. From my guess, I would say it was their way of saying hello out here.

I made my way through the airport towards baggage claim. It was nothing spectacular from what I was seeing. It wasn't the size of Tokyo, which was good. It was simple and easy to navigate. *Cool beans,* I thought. I finally made it over to baggage claim, yet I didn't see anyone here waiting for me. I remember the message I got, telling me that someone would be waiting for me, ready to do some G shit. I quickly looked around to see that unlike many airports, this baggage claim was separated from the rest of the airport. The big doors led out to the common area, so whoever was gonna surprise me would have to wait. Twelve minutes passed until the carousel finally got to moving. Bag after bag was coming, and person after person was grabbing. This wasn't a big flight number wise, so why my stuff wasn't seen yet, I had no clue.

After about 10 agonizing minutes, I started to get worried that my stuff got lost. Great, I thought. I fly overseas and my shit ends up somewhere in the Pacific Ocean. As I ended up being the last one left, and ready to snap, two lowly bags came out onto the carousel. Man I swear this was God messing with me. I waited for them to make their way around, scooping them up, making sure nothing was tampered with or anything. I made my way over to the customs desk for them to check out my stuff.

"Hafa Adai. Military?," the local islander asked.

"Naw. Contractor for the government, though."

"Okay, Okay," he said with a smile on his face. He stamped my papers.

"Welcome to Guam and enjoy." I grabbed them joints and headed for the doors. As I made it in front of them, I took a deep breath and closed my eyes. *Here we go,* I thought. I pushed my way through. As I rounded past a set of chairs, my bags and my mouth dropped. I was greeted with a smile that brought me back to my early 20's.

"Kamilah!!!," I yelled. All she did was smile even more.

"Hi Lamar," talking with a grin that stretched the seven seas. I walked over to hug her, impervious to my bags.

"What are you doing over here?"

"I told you that I'd be waiting on you when you got here. I knew if I sounded like a nigga that you would have no clue who it was. I work as a contractor on the Air Force base as well, but I'm bout to leave. You taking one of my friend's positions. Let's get your bags and roll up out of here."

Man this was the shock of all shocks. I met this girl years ago while stopping through one of the old ratchet young folk joints called club 702. We talked for a good minute and eventually hit it off. After a couple of dates to the movies and chillin', we eventually started to catch feelings for one another. However, she couldn't pursue anything further, seeing that she was heading out of state for college. Now it was deja vu all over again, except she was going back stateside.

Banging wasn't the word to describe this girl. Perfection was more like it. She was 5'7, 140 pounds of all thickness. Flat stomach, big ass, nice breasts, with long hair. Most important of all though, she was well educated. It was amazing after losing contact all these years, we were finally back in each other's presence. We made it to the car and it was like being with my best friend the way we were talking.

"So I know you surprised...but are you surprised?" Her smile followed those words and made me blush.

"Man..........a..........like........I really wasn't expecting you. I honestly thought I would never see you again. What's the last seven to eight years been like?"

"Well, school, obviously. Major opportunities. Great money. A life that only certain people dream of." We got to the light on the main road and that's when she hit me.

"But......but........one thing I don't got is someone to ride this out with." I looked at her strangely. I knew she was a good hearted person from our past interactions, so how she didn't have a man was shocking.

"So hold up. How you not got a man?"

"It's me, Lamar. All me. I'm intimidating. I'm independent, but I don't pretend like I don't yearn to have a man in my presence. Like...I'm almost 30. Only stupid females at this age brag about being single or that they're so independent that they don't need a man in their lives. Hell, you don't need a car to get from point A to point B, but it's nice to have around because it makes things a whole lot easier." She continued as I soaked in every word she was spitting out.

"When I saw your name on the list for new personnel coming to the base, I thought, wow, he is really coming here. So...I'm not asking to be in a relationship with you, cause obviously it can't happen cause I'm leaving. What I am asking is that we can stay in each other's lives to help balance each other out. I'm not crazy to think you're not gonna explore this island and see a lot of women who catch your eye. You just got here and I know how it is. I was exploring myself when I first came. Just know, though...that.....I really wish I could see where we could actually go and if it can be meaningful like all those years ago when we were barely 20 years old. That's all I'm saying." The word impressive was an understatement. What woman talked like this? Not any woman that I could think of.

"So where are you taking me?," I asked.

"Well, I know your condo is ready, but seeing how it's past one o'clock on a Friday morning, I figured you could crash at my place. Plus, you don't have to check in 'til Monday, and I informed our supervisor that I know you so you'll be in good hands. Is that cool with you?" I don't even know why she asked that.

"Cool beans." She giggled.

"What the hell is cool beans?"

"I dunno, yo," I said with a laugh. "I just one day out of the blue started saying it. I don't know where it came from, but it became a part of my vocab." We kept the jokes and laughs going all the way to the island's main strip.

"What's this area called?"

"Tumon," she said. "This is where all the clubs, high end shopping and restaurants exists. Plus, it's where the congregation of ratchet Navy and Air Force chicks meet." I laughed my ass off as I took in the sights. G-Spot I saw. Well, that had to be the strip club. Hotels galore were down here. Yea, I could tell that this was their money making tourist area. Finally, we made a left turn into a parking lot.

"C'mon out. Let's get something to eat. You're gonna like it. Trust me." I got out the car and it just felt good. It had to be at least 80, however, it was a cool, night time 80 degrees, and not any of those scorching Vegas 80 degree nights. The Kracked Egg restaurant is what I walked into. Hmmm? I was a big weight room buff, and Lord knows I needed my GAINZ while out here. This looked like the perfect place. We walked on in and sat down. I scanned through the menu, looking at what I wanted to devour besides this fine piece of work sitting across from me. This corned beef omelette looked about right. I swear I could eat that stuff all day long. For a quick second, I thought I was back in the D at Louie's. The waitress came over and we ordered up the grub. The night was shared with stories of Kamilah in her college days, and mines of my come ups in Vegas since she had left, however, I left out the details of everything that had happened within the last two months. I know it wasn't healthy to hold stuff like that in, and she was someone that I could confide in. However, I was trying to process it out of my head, and I felt right now it was best to keep it in. An hour or so passed, and before you knew it, it was almost three o'clock in the morning.

"You ready?," she said. With a stuffed, satisfied look on my face, I let out a slow and lethargic

"Yeaaaaa." I was good and sleepy now. We got back in the car and headed up the hill.

"So how far is your crib from here?"

"About another two or three minutes." We made a right near what looked like their version of an amusement park and hit a quick left into a condo complex that made me say oh shit. This girl really was doing it big, and this was major proof. I ain't gone lie. For a quick second, I felt intimidated a lil bit. She parked the car, I grabbed my stuff and followed her into the elevator. We took it all the way up to the top floor. That's how I knew it was gonna be a smooth dwelling. Descending off the elevator, the hallway had a smell of success. I don't know what I was more impressed by. The sight of this great living, or the sight of her perfectly shaped ass in those jeans she was wearing.

They said if you spend your time chasing ass, you will end up with shit. Well, this was one I would chase cause trust, wasn't nothing shitty about her personality or lifestyle. Walking into her condo behind her was like walking into MTV cribs. She definitely had this place decked out. A big ol' 65 inch flat screen was perched on the living room wall. Clean, tan carpet lined the floors into her dining room. Her kitchen was pure hardwood with marble countertops. Most of all though, it was clean.

"Hey? Lamar?" I barely even heard her because I was in such awe of her place. "This is your room over here." I lugged those bags over to enter what looked like a mini place in itself.

"You got your own bathroom, TV, all that. I already put out towels, a wash cloth and toothpaste is in the medicine cabinet. Make yourself at home." She grabbed my face and kissed me on my forehead.

"Goodnight," she uttered as she walked off. I was officially on ten, but I couldn't show it. I plopped down on my bed thinking how great it was to have a fresh start. A shower could wait until the morning as far as I was concerned. That was until I caught a whiff of myself and the smell hit me.

"Fuck this shit!!!," I said out loud. I needed to go wash my ass. I was smelling like I had sat in a tub of hot baby Llama lung juice. I guess that's what all that flying and moving around will do to you. I cranked that shower up immediately! The water was warm and pouring off me ever so gently. As I finished up, I wrapped the towel around myself and curled up under the fan that was in my room. Things were quiet out in the house, so I assumed that Kamilah had went to sleep. I sat there in my thoughts. I started to dwell on the past. I had a problem with doing this. It was sort of like being bi polar. One minute, I was cool and free. The next, it was dark and twisted. It was either what I had or what I didn't have anymore and my mind would start twisting and turning. Quickly, I pulled out my IPOD and let some old Big Mike turn up through my Beats.

"Can it be it's all a dream...all a dream...all a dream..all a dreammm." This song slowly but surely started to put me back in an easy state of mind. Truthfully, this was all a dream, except this one had turned into reality. All I had left to do was make sure that the dream didn't turn into a nightmare. I fell asleep like a baby.

"Breakfast is ready." I rolled over to see Kamilah in the doorway, in some sweats and a wife beater. Claude have mercy!!! If God had made anything prettier, he had for damn sure kept it to himself.

"Oh thank you sweetheart," I said with breath that smelled like I chewed on a bag of 1000 camel assholes. "I'll be there in a minute." She walked out and I plopped back down on the bed. I looked over at the clock to see it was 9:57. I was honestly still messed up by the time change, so I wasn't too keen on anything right now. I went to Colgate my mouth up thoroughly, followed by a nice facial cleanse. I threw on some shorts and a beater, and headed into the kitchen.

"Wow girl, you ain't have to do this." She just smiled as she flipped an omelette over.

"There's your plate on the table." I turned around to see grits, links, a ham and cheese omelette, hash browns, corned beef hash and a biscuit with strawberry jelly spread throughout the middle. How the hell wasn't she locked down again? I went and sat down, waiting for her to finish making her plate. She joined me.

"You wanna pray over the food?" Man if this didn't turn me on even more, I don't know what would. You'd be surprised how impressive it is for a woman to ask you to pray over the food. I agreed, we bowed our heads, said a prayer and commenced to operation smash.

"So is there anything you are gonna show me today?"

"Well," as she took another gulp of her omelette, "I figured I'd take you to Andersen today, let you meet some of the folks you'll be working with."

"Do you work in the same department as me?" She laughed.

"Oh no. You're a computer tech. I'm just here as a HAZMAT technician for 7th fleet. All my primary work is done between here and Japan. I run the whole CHRIMP program for this area. Trust, I sometimes wish that I was sitting behind a computer. The only thing we share is the same supervisor." I was even more impressed.

"So...I know it was super late last night and we didn't really get in depth, but what made you take the job over here, besides the money of course?"

I stalled for a minute, getting a few bites of this bomb ass corned beef hash. My answer could be simple, but I wanted her to know the truth, seeing that she had opened up to me.

"I was hesitant at first. I had to talk with my aunt to get her advice and she said I should do it. I mean, it wasn't gaining her approval, but she has always given me great advice. So I took the job, and slowly after that, a slew of things started happening. Ummm.......I went back home to Detroit and my first cousin was killed directly in my face. I broke up with my fiancee, which I never wanted to happen, but some issues just couldn't be resolved. My mom and I started having problems with our relationship. Also, the day before I left, I almost was killed in a robbery gone wrong at a liquor store. So to say this job is just a new experience would mean I was lying to you. I mean it is, but now, I feel like I needed this so I could find myself again. I mean, out of everything that happened, my break up was the worse.

You give yourself to someone for almost three years, and all of a sudden, it disappears in the blink of an eye. We grew apart, letting some differences get the best of us. Looking back, I was spiteful as hell to her. I regret it now. She didn't deserve what I did to her afterwards. That's something I will have to live with for the rest of my life. I should've just let that shit go and let us both be. However, I became the asshole. The one part of me that I absolutely hate to see. That's why this new chapter is so important to me. That, my family life and just stuff that I had to endure seeing makes being over here even more important. And that's it." She stared a hole through me with a look of shock in her eyes.

"Commere," she said as she stood up. I walked over and we embraced in a hug. She caressed my head with her hands as if to tell me that it would be okay now. I hadn't been hugged like this by a woman in a long time. It actually felt more intimate than sympathetic.

"Let me tell you something," as she grabbed my face. "In life, you have a choice or two. You can either learn from your past and move on. Or.......you can stay stuck in it, and never progress. The choice is yours. The man I see though, I know he knows what he has to do." She kissed me on my forehead.

"Let's finish eating so we can go handle things today." We sat back down. What I thought would be a quiet breakfast turned into a very upbeat one, as she ensured our conversations stayed on something positive and focused on staying up. If it's one thing I had learned from living in Vegas, it's that you upgrade, not downgrade. Sometimes, when you think you downgrade, you actually upgrade, and vice versa. Right now, in this moment, I could see that my upgrade had occurred.

We finished up breakfast, got dressed and rolled out. As soon as I stepped outside to the lot, it felt like the devil cut loose in my face. It was hot as dog balls out here.

"Is this the temp everyday 'Milah?"

"Yea. It's about 105 in the day and it don't get below 80 ever for a low." Man this was like being in Vegas all over again, minus the humidity.

"I'm gonna take you over to your condo building first so you can meet with your landlord, check out your place and all that good stuff."

Cool beans, I thought. We hopped up in her Mercedes S class and peeled out. I still had to go pick up my whip, but that could wait. I wanted to see the life that I would be living for the next two years. After about a ten minute drive, we headed down a side street that wasn't too far off the strip. The closer we got, I could see a Sheraton Hotel booming above the landscape. I could tell by the giant S that even a blind man couldn't miss it. That thing was huge. Right before we headed to the road to get to the hotel, she made a sharp left. In the distance, I seen a building about eight stories high. As we got to the guard shack, where no guard was present, I seen the sign. Alupang Cove Condominiums. From the front, it really didn't look like anything spectacular. We parked and headed into the office that was right there as soon as you walked in. Inside, there were two women. A young girl, pretty, but hefty in size. Next, a woman with long hair who looked like she was in her 60's.

"Linda?"

"HI KAMILAH!!!" I had taken these two had met before with the greeting they gave each other.

"This is the new tenant I was telling you about. Lamar, Linda. Linda, Lamar." We shook hands and again, I was greeted with Hafa Adai. I still didn't know what the hell it meant.

"Well, if you're ready, I'll take you up to your home for the next two years. Cool?"

"Cool," I responded. We took the elevator up to the fourth floor. As we got off and followed Linda, I realized that this place was an old hotel converted into some condos.

"This is you, all the way at the end. Number 416." *Condo #416,* I thought. *The crackhouse* as I said in my head naming it, because I planned to have things cracking off up in here. As the door opened, I became perplexed. I had seen a lot of things in my day, but what I was witnessing at this moment almost took the breath out of my body.

"Look around and tell me what you think?" I didn't even hear Linda's words, as all I noticed was the breath taking view from my balcony of the Pacific Ocean. I had never in my life seen something this amazing. I opened the patio door and stepped outside. I could smell the aroma of greatness in the air. I felt like The Rock. Do you smell what's cookin? I indeed did, and what was cooking was pure life.

"Lamar? I take it you like it?" I turned back into the house.

"Linda, I love it." With a quick glance around this one bedroom, I seen that everything was right where I needed it to be. All I needed to do was unpack my clothes out of the boxes and I was on my way.

"Alright, well, I'll come back Monday so you can sign your paperwork. Everything is already on. They paid for your lights, internet and all that. All you need to do is get a cell phone and you will be okay." Linda waived by to us both, leaving us to be.

"So how you like your first impression of Guam, Lamar?"

"I LOVE IT!!! It's like Heaven dropped down on Earth and I ended up residing in it!!!" Kamilah was excited for me as much as I was excited for myself.

"C'mon, lets go head up north. I'll take you to get your car on Monday. I got you on your first weekend." We left the crackhouse and peeled out onto Route 1. This was the main road going through the island. She showed me different joints along the way, including Micronesia Mall. It didn't look impressive, but for this island it was. The farther north we got, the more desolate it became. I seen less and less of buildings, and more and more of green jungle type atmospheres. She said wild caribou and pigs ran rampant out here. I was just hoping that one didn't cross into the road and mess us both up.

"Andersen Air Force Base, huh?"

"Yep," Kamilah said. Now I know that I was in the car with a beauty, but Lord knows that I knew about the Air Force. They say there was no such thing as an ugly woman in the Air Force. From working with them in Vegas, they were absolutely right. Judging from the gate guard at the gate, I found that definitely to be true in Guam as well. Shorty looked very, very ripe in her uniform. We pulled off down a long to death road that seemed like it was going straight to hell. After about 15 minutes of driving, we finally reached the logistics building.

"Have your papers ready with your I.D.," 'Milah told me. I had everything in hand, waiting to see what my next step in life was gonna be. As we entered, we went through an I.D. check along with walking through a metal detector. We reached the reception desk where a fellow civilian was working.

"Hi, I'm Lamar Atteley, the new hire as a security system analyst."

"Hello Mr. Atteley, we've been expecting you. If you walk down this hall to your left, there will be the office of Mr. Tom Wilder, the head of the whole intel department. I'm Suzanne and welcome aboard." We shook hands and Kamilah went back to the car to wait for me as I went to talk with my new boss. I entered his office and we hit it off well. He was a fellow Midwesterner who hailed from Ohio. He spent 25 years on active duty as a computer analyst for the Air Force, so he knew his work and knew it well. The only knock I had on him was that he was a fan of Ohio State. Other than that, he was cool beans. He informed me that I would start Tuesday and that I would have no problem fitting in with the team, made up of former military and highly qualified civilians. I walked out of the building with confidence, giving Suzanne a thumbs up as I left.

"Hafa Adai," she said as I departed. I still didn't know what that shit meant. I made it back to the car with Kamilah.

"How was it?," she asked.

"It was great!!! It went way better than planned."

"Good. Now, let's go chill for the rest of this weekend." We peeled down that long road to hell, back off base and headed south.

"How you liking it so far Lamar?" I looked out the window and just smiled.

"I mean, I love it so far. I got a good job, got good weather, got you. So shit, I'm straight." She looked at me as we got to a stoplight.

"Yea, you do have me. I just hope I can have you back in return." In all honesty, I really didn't get that, even though she expressed her feelings to me when I first got here. Usually, when a woman wants something, she does whatever it takes to get it. However, it was crazy because she was gonna allow me to do me. In a way I was playing tug of war with my heart. I could go easy and build something with this girl. Or, I could soy my royal oats all over this island. Deep down, I knew what would be the smart thing to do. At the same time, I wanted to be a man. Plus, long distance would be hard.

"You wanna go out tonight?," I asked her, like I knew what the hell to do over here.

"Yea that's cool. We can sit on the beach at your complex, watch the sunset and then go chill at this joint called The

Tree Bar." I was down, she was down and this looked like the makings of a good damn night.

The day was spent back at her place laughing, joking and talking about random instances in our lives that molded us. One incident I shared with her that I had never told anyone else was that of a death that brought more than distraught to my life. The year was 2000. It was a typical summer for me. I had weight lifting sessions in the morning and conditioning for football season in the afternoons. I was about to begin my junior year starting in the fall. I was truly on a high. Even more of a reason to be on a high was that my mans Clarence was coming out to be on the team. We all called him "SMURF." He was a cool ass dude from my side of the blocks and got along with everybody. One Saturday, as usual, we met up at the local Boys and Girls Club, along with the rest of the hood. We hooped from damn near 12 o'clock in the afternoon all the way to six in the evening. Tired and drained, us as kids, we didn't take our tails home immediately. We posted up outside of the club just choppin it up. As it got well beyond 7:00, everybody started to go their separate ways. Me and SMURF were the last ones left.

"Aight Mar, be easy my dude." We dapped up.

"I'll see you at practice on Monday," I told him. I walked home and thought nothing else of it. It was a great day with my boys. As a teenager in this environment, getting black kids together to be constructive and not destructive was a blessing. Sunday went by with a blur. I did the typical of going to church and eating up my mom's Sunday cooking. Then...then came Monday. Full pads was set for 12 that afternoon, so I swung by the club to chill for a while. When I got there, I saw my boy Le'Andre chillin by the window. I went over, fucking with him as usual. Today though, he wasn't having it.

"What's wrong bruh?" With tears in his eyes, he told me five words that stopped my heartbeat.

"SMURF got shot dead man." My blood circulation stopped. My breathing seemed to cease. Nothing else mattered at this point. What I just heard, I truly couldn't believe. SMURF was gone. He was shot seven times execution style, not to far from his home. There were a lot of deaths that affected me in my teenage years. This however took on a whole new meaning. I remember walking into the football facility that day, debating on how I was gonna break the news. I walked into the training room, where Donta, our star running back was getting treated before practice, along with a few others. Coach Worowz, probably the coolest coach we had, was in there as well.

"Coach..ummm...SMURF was shot last night." He gave me a stunned look, and everything stopped.

"Is he okay?" The look on my face said it all. They knew before I said it.

"Nah." I walked out and headed into the locker room. The mood got somber real quick when the rest of the team found out. We had the shittiest practice that I could ever remember that day. I don't think our head coach understood, but there were things bigger than football at this moment. We were about to bury another brother of ours. This was becoming a common ritual here in the D and it sucked majorly. Life was so much more than which way you broke your hat or what hood you lived in. However, in our environment, it was hard to ever see anything positive. After that conversation, things really began to turn emotion wise. I could see she was even more into me than ever before. As for me though, I didn't want to lead her on. I wasn't ready for such a woman. Considering what I had went through before I left the states, to just my all out maturity level, I wasn't ready for her. She was too good of a woman to mess over. I went back to my room to catch what I call a thought nap. I was tired to a degree, but my mind was still racing. Time continued to drift and I finally did.

"Lamar. Lamar!!!" I turned over as 'Milah was shaking the hell outta me. "Throw on some clothes. We're going to watch the sunset at your place." I struggled to get up. I still swore I was on American time. I threw on my shorts from earlier and a beater. I tried to be loose while getting my thug look on at the same time. I rubbed down my arms and chest with baby oil so all 15 of my tattoos were standing out. Some niggas might call it gay, but I was comfortable in my skin. Plus, it was never a piece of pussy that I ever came across that I didn't like.

"And why the hell are you coming out lookin like a reflector lens?" She had jokes I see.

"Nah. I just wanna bring the tats out a little bit." She shook her head and just laughed.

"Boy, C'mon." We rolled out the crib and onto the Tumon strip. It wasn't sunset yet, but the lights started to come on and I could tell it looked like a gem during the night. We cruised with the windows halfway down, laughing, talking and enjoying some R. Kelly. We made it to my complex with ease, sliding into parking slot 64. We exited out, and as we met each other at the back of the car, she reached out and grabbed my hand.

"What are you trying to make me feel Milah? I know the obvious, but I don't know."

"Just walk and enjoy it," she said. She had gotten real serious with those words. I knew this girl was wanting something more. What I couldn't understand though was why with me. Besides the little history we had, we weren't involved with each other long enough to establish a connection. We made it around to the back of the building. The pool was glistening, yet empty. The sky was starting to dim a little bit and its colors began to create a painting on the ocean surface.

"Take a seat," she said. Asses on the grass, we both looked out at the sun, slowly dropping beneath the surface and illuminating the sky into a spectrum.

"What do you see Lamar?" I really didn't know how to answer that question.

"Ummmmm.......a bunch of colors coming together to make one great showing." There was dead silence. Then, 'Milah said something that struck the depths of a brother.

"That's right. Many colors. Many colors creating one masterpiece. Like us. We're together. I grabbed your hand so we could feel what it's like to be connected. I dunno Lamar. I went off to college and thought about you a lot. You made a big impact on me in such a very short amount of time. When I saw you that day at the airport, I asked myself what if. Now, I'm hoping, but I know the real. Like I told you, I can't control what you do, but I wanted to make my intentions clear. More importantly, when I leave, I just want you to be careful with the decisions you make. I see so much in you it doesn't even seem real." Kamilah then laid her head on my shoulder and I just sat there in silence. No woman had ever said anything like that to me. I looked up at the sky. The colors were just as if God were painting things himself. Nothing else was said as we just sat there until the last bit of sun disappeared. Even then, we continued to sit.

"You ready?," she asked, as it was now completely dark.

"Yea, let's ride." As I got up, I helped her up. I kept a hold of her hand, and she just looked at me and smiled. I was so scared to commit to another woman. I did wanna explore this island, but I didn't want her, or another good woman to slip away. Damn, I wish life wasn't this damn complicated. We made it back to the car and began our way back towards the strip.

"So why did you keep a grip on my hand? Be honest."

As I gazed out the window, I answered, "I dunno. It just felt good because I haven't been with a woman since my engagement was broke off. I'm gone be honest 'Milah. I like you. I like you a helluva lot. At the same time, I don't wanna be the dick who messes up something good. I came over here with the intention of not giving a damn about any woman, all because of how my last relationship ended. Right now, I don't want to put you in a situation with a mentally unstable nigga." There was dead silence. She turned at the light by Payless Supermarket, which was the back road to the strip. Suddenly, she made a right into the shopping plaza and parked in front of a lowly coffee shop.

"Come in with me Lamar." Her voice was very somber when she said that. Great, I thought. I had ruined the moment and the mood. She walked in while I hesitated outside. *Java Hut Coffee Shop*, I said to myself. I chuckled a bit as I thought about Star Wars for a quick minute. My mind immediately went back to the matter at hand. I walked in to see 'Milah choppin it up with the woman behind the counter. The place was empty minus us.

"Ruby, this is Lamar. Lamar, Ruby." We shook hands and greeted each other.

"So you're the guy Kamilah has been raving about."

"Excuse me," I said.

"Yea. She told me she had a close friend who was coming. You guys look cute together." I was trying not to smile, but I had no choice. I liked compliments like that.

"Thanks. Yea........we do look great together." Laughter burst out, but I heard in 'Milah's laugh that it was one of just trying to play things off.

"We're closed, but she's a regular, so I made you both some food to go. I'll go check on it." As Ruby went back to the kitchen, I looked over at 'Milah, but no eye contact was given back. I knew what the problem was, but I didn't want to be the one to say anything.

"Thanks Ruby. Have a good night," she uttered as she grabbed the food and headed for the door. I waved to Ruby and followed out behind 'Milah. As I got in the car behind her, I could feel tension in the air that was as thick as a pot of grits. I sat there, watching her take the paper off a sandwich.

"So how's the Tree Bar that we're going to?" She took a bite, not even paying me any mind.

"I don't feel like going anymore." As I opened my mouth to speak again, she just cut me off. "You know Lamar. You say we look great together, but you say you are mentally unstable. That thinking, that type of thinking right there, is what's gonna cause you to miss out on something great. I know you are better than that, so that's why it's upsetting that I'm hearing you speak such utter bullshit."

I didn't really know what to do. I figured I had killed the mood, but damn. It sounded more like I had killed our friendship. I sat quiet like a kid who was in the corner for timeout, waiting patiently as she finished her sandwich. Once she did, she started up the car and peeled off. The ride back to her condo was a silent and uneasy one. We left earlier in the evening great friends. Now, I didn't even know if we were going to speak again. She immediately went to her room, shutting the door behind her. I stared at the door from the doorway of my room. I was saddened and hurt that I broke this girl's heart. I said what I thought she wanted to hear. However, this just proved lying to make things sound good did more bad than good. Sometimes it works. In this case, it backfired. I entered my room and shut the door. Looking at the clock, I seen it was only 7:58. It was early as ever, and I was stuck in the house. I plopped on the bed and just stared at the ceiling. I didn't know what I was expecting to happen. I guess I was waiting for some magical man to jump down and say everything was gonna be okay. As I really focused and zoned out, I heard noises from outside my room. I got up and creaked open the door to hear the sounds of what sounded like crying. I slowly inched my way towards her door to place my ear against the wood. She was ballin and ballin hard. I felt like an ass. This was terrible. This girl put aside everything to help me. Hell she even talked me up as a great man to some people. Now, one false statement caused a whirlwind of hurt. I knocked on her door and entered in. She didn't even hear me because she was crying so loud. She was sprawled across the bed, face down and seriously hurting. I sat down next to her, caressing her back slowly with my hand. She looked up, wiping her eyes.

"Hi," she muffled.

"Look, 'Milah. I said what I thought you wanted to hear. I was wrong. I am sorry for hurting you like I did. I never meant that. I just don't want to give you, or any woman an incomplete man." She raised up to sit next to me. Grabbing my face, she kissed me so softly on the lips.

"I don't see you as incomplete. I see you as a man who needs to be reminded of how special he is. That's it." I just looked at her. No woman, not even my ex had made me feel like she did with words.

"I don't know what to say. What do you want me to say?" With a deep breath, she gave me her response.

"Nothing. Your look says it all." She kissed me on the forehead. "Get some you time with the TV. I'll be okay." She rolled over and laid on her side, not saying anything else. With disdain, I left the room and went outside on her balcony. I sat in that chair looking out into the warm, star lit Guam night. It sounded lively down below. Inside my soul, though, I was lower than the roots under a tree. How did I rekindle and mess up a friendship in less than 24 hours? Only a fool could do such a thing, and I proved that I was indeed one. I looked over at the other empty chair on the balcony, wishing and hoping that she would come out here and join me. I wasn't depressed, but I didn't feel good either. I walked back in the house and straight to the fridge. I grabbed some strawberry jelly and some wheat bread. I found the peanut butter up in the cabinet and commenced to making sandwiches. After making four of em and putting em on the plate, I started putting everything up, expecting for a quiet night in my quarters.

"Tell me a story." I turned around to see Kamilah standing in the doorway to the kitchen.

"Excuse me," I said, like I didn't hear her the first time.

"Tell me a story." I kind of chuckled.

"I don't know what to tell you. What do you wanna know?"

"Tell me about November 4, 2010." The lump in my throat damn near dropped to my feet. I stared a hole through her thinking how in the hell did she know.

"Let's sit," I told her. We sat down at the kitchen table. The time was 9:30 on the dot. I didn't even know that much time had passed. I looked dead into her eyes and poured out my soul.

"There I was, laid up in a hospital bed, laughing and joking with my family. It was early, like seven something in the morning type early. They said my surgery would be around nine o'clock. Well jokes flew, time flew, until the docs finally came to send my family off and wheel me into the surgery room. I looked at those lights differently once I got in there. I thought like all hell it would be the last thing I would see. The heart ain't the easiest thing to deal with. Not in a relationship, nor in real life. I had been having problems, and they had found some irregularity in one of my heart valves. They were gonna do what they needed to do to fix a brother. As I got put in the room, the doctors who wheeled me in left. I was left alone. It had to be for at least 30 minutes. In that time, I was scared shitless. I didn't know what to think. Finally, a nurse came in to prep me for surgery. It was cool. She was an older black lady, and she was making me feel at ease. Then a male nurse walked in, talking 'bout, "Sir, I have to shave you." Ain't this bout a bitch, I thought. It sucked cause if I did die on the table, the last image I would have from this earthly life is a man shaving my balls. Time seemed to stand still. Finally, the docs came in. The anesthesia was put into my veins and I slowly started to fade. Three hours later, I was up and being wheeled to a room. They had me lay absolutely still for five hours, no higher than a 30 degree rise on the bed. They were not wanting me to bleed out, seeing that they went through the femoral arteries in my legs. Once I was finally able to get up out of bed and walk, I had a brand new appreciation on life." I took a deep breath, because it felt like I was reliving that entire experience for a moment.

"But how did you know?," I asked. The moment felt tense as we stared at each other.

"When you care about somebody Lamar, you always make sure they are okay. I know people. So when you went down, I was devastated and praying like never before that you were okay. I just care about you, and I'm kind of scared that I care too much at times." She once again had me feeling a certain type of way.

"Can I hug you?" I know it was the corniest thing ever to say, but I couldn't think of nothing else. How a woman could have this much love for you was damn near unheard of. We raised up, sharing a moment, looking into each other's souls through touch. As we embraced each other, I closed my eyes, thinking about the only other time in my life that a hug was the equivalent of a million dollars.

My grandma back in 2005 had a health scare. She had intestinal hernia. She couldn't have a bowel movement, and it eventually led to an infection. Word from the docs was that emergency surgery had to be performed or she would face the ultimate price. Death. I flew in from Vegas the day of the surgery. As I got off the plane, I was in a world of confusion. I had been in the air for a few hours, so anything could have happened. When I saw my pops, he let me know that she was good. I got home, dropped my bags off and raced to St. John's hospital in my daddy's truck. I got there, immediately seeing my mama downstairs in the gift shop.

"MA!!! How's Grandma?!" She turned around, stunned by my loud voice.

"Well, welcome home. She doing fine. She up, but she still got tubes in her." I got on the elevator with moms, and I swore it was going slower than a Rex Grossman led Bears offense. As the doors opened to the ICU, she directed me to the room. As I entered, I seen my uncles and my aunt. There she was, lying in a bed, tubes all in her, looking real grim. That's how it looked from my perspective. As she turned her head to notice me, she smiled. I burst out with tears of joy. My grandma was my world. Had it not been for her on many rough nights when my parents were going at each other's throats, I don't know where I would be in life. A few days later, she was released out of the hospital. As I seen her take her first steps, I gave her the biggest hug known to man. The only other time I hugged her this hard was when I hit my leg on a small pipe sticking out of the ground when I was nine.

I ran back to her house where she was looking at me out the window. She gave me a big ol' hug to let me know it was okay. Then she grabbed some cotton balls and peroxide and proceeded to heal her grandbaby. Those were the best times of my life. She died in 2007, on a lowly September 19th night. I felt like my heart had been ripped out of my chest. I withered away on my green couch at the time, and felt like God was punishing me for all the negative shit I had done over the course of my life. It took months, and I mean months, to get back to myself. Four to be exact. When January 2008 came around, I finally started to feel at peace. I realized she was at peace, so I obtained peace for myself.

"Let's lay together." Why did I tell her this? It was simple. I needed comfort. Don't ever let men fool you as if they don't enjoy holding a woman. Sometimes, we need it more than them. We got to the bedroom, lied down and just stared at each other. No words were said, but they didn't need to be. The fingers I ran through her hair did enough talking. I kissed her on the forehead as her face lit up with excitement. I can't remember when we fell asleep, but I will never forget the glow that we seen in each other's eyes.

5 SHIT IS REAL

Two weeks had almost passed. I was settled into my condo, in which I called crackhouse 416. I got my car, my island stickers, all that. I hadn't done much to explore this joint besides the little bit that I did with Kamilah. We were now back on our regular work schedules and hadn't hung out for two weekends. It was gravy, though. We kept up through text messages and phone conversations. Really, she was preppin' to leave. She would come in during the morning and then be gone in the afternoon. I swear I was being a stubborn ass.

I knew she wanted to do right by me, but I was still in man whore mode. I wanted to see what I could knock down here first before committing to someone serious. Here it was, May 25th on this side of the world. I was chilling at the crib, ready to enjoy my second weekend on the island. I got off early that day, two o'clock to be exact. *Fuck it,* I thought. I'll cruise down to the southern tip of the island, AGAT, and see what was up down there. I mean, it wasn't hard to find your way around here. One main road was all that went through here, and every side street would eventually take you back to Route 1. I hopped in the whip and cranked up the speakers, knocking one of my man's Joenigma joints. He was a lyrical cat out of North Carolina that I met on the West while I was residing in Vegas. His music put my mind at ease as I made the turn headed towards Route 1. Things were cool, calm and collective. It was hot as a set of monkey nuts in the jungle, but this was Guam. I couldn't expect anything else. I turned onto Route 1, bobbin' my head to the beat. This felt like one of those Vegas late night rides, minus the darkness and the bright lights. There wasn't much sightseeing, but I took in everything I saw just to get a feel for what was around here. I hadn't really paid attention in the time I was here so I took advantage of this opportunity. I got to the light. As I glanced to my right, I noticed a small cemetery. Who in the hell would put a cemetery in this weird spot? It beats the hell outta me, but I guessed that's how they rolled. The light turned green. I peeled off, not thinking much of anything.

Then.........***BOOM!!!*** Glass shattered everywhere. The crunch of the metal sounded like my car had got balled up and thrown away like a piece of paper. My body jerked in every which way. Airbags deployed. Stunned, I saw white mist everywhere. I'm a nigga and it didn't take rocket science for me to put two and two together. White mist usually equals smoke. Where there is smoke, there is fire. I banged my shoulder repeatedly until the car door opened and I literally fell out. My left arm was completely numb as I regained my balance and stumbled over to the parking lot of one of the local joints. Once my focus came back, I saw everything. A black Ford F-150, lifted up, with a custom bumper guard. It looked like it hadn't been scratched. My shit though was completely totaled.

"Bruh, you okay?" I aint know who the hell this dude was, but I was glad someone was there. "I called the medics already. Just stand off to the side and be cool." I wanted to say something back, but I was too pissed and stunned to respond. As he guided me to the side and more and more people came out of nearby buildings, I saw the cat who hit me. He was a local cat, no more than 22 I would assume. Him and his ugly bitch was in the car. She was looking scared as ever while he had a what the fuck look on his face.

"Bruh, I'm Tony." I looked up to this short brother, not knowing what to think of him, but just glad he was there.

"Lamar," I said with pain written all over me.

"Listen," he said, "I'm a tow truck driver and my brother owns the company. I'll take care of you mane. I seen everything. Just trust me on this." I didn't wanna believe anything this dude was saying, but what did I have to lose at this point, I thought. As I heard the medics coming up the street, I told him, "Sure." We exchanged numbers and Tony began the process of putting my car on the tow bed, seeing that he had his truck with him. The paramedics arrived along with the police. They were interviewing several people while EMT's tended to me.

"I think something is severely wrong with my arm, doc." As they began to work on my left arm, one of them put my fears to rest.

"You got mobility so it's not broken. Maybe a sprain or a contusion, but it's not broken at all. Let's get you in the ambulance and take you to the hospital."

"HELL NAW!!!," I shouted. "I just got here on island, sir. I can't break the bank for an ambulance ride yet. Y'all charge an arm and a leg for oxygen." All three of them chuckled.

"Sir, you're a government employee I assume, correct?" I nodded my head up and down, still appalled that they actually asked me to get in that damn traveling expense. "Well, you know you're covered medically, and that includes ambulance rides. So in lamens terms, it's free. Now, do you wanna go to the hospital to get X-rays?" When he put it like that, I only had one response.

"Yea, fuck it. Y'all can gone head and load me up." We shared a laugh in that moment, but immediately my mind started going back to a dark place.

We had a barber in our city named Paul. I was very young at the time, but all my older cousins and all the elders from the hood raved about him. He was a short, light skinned brother with a head full of waves. He had been tutored by another great, Mr. Tau Baraka, a revolutionary type man who did wonderful things in the black community for his city. I remember one day sitting at home, I was in my early teens, and I had the urge to walk down to the liquor store and get me some chic-o-sticks, lemon heads, a $0.25 juice and some flamin' hots. As I was waiting in line, I over heard the conversation taking place between two cats from the East Side.

"Man bruh, what happened to Paul was fucked up mane. All the good niggas die young." As he placed his cash on the countertop to pay for his forty, his partner responded.

"Yea G. It could've been any one of us on that road. Folks gone be missed severely." They then both walked out. I crept up to the counter scared as ever, for what reason I don't know. Somehow, I felt like I had known Paul, even though he never cut my hair. As I got my stuff and returned home, I cut on the 5 o'clock news. There it was, the first story that made it on the news. He had collided with the back of a semi truck that was stalled on the side of the road. More than likely, some idiot who didn't know how to drive caused him to swerve to avoid a wreck and he ended up being in one.

It was sad to see. It was a memory that always stuck with me. I know the barbershop is a place for the black community to come together and release every bit of energy we have through conversations. However, it is rare that a barber could touch the lives of so many from every side of the city. I personally didn't know Paul, nor had I ever met him. Judging from the reaction of those two brothers at the liquor store, and the many more I would encounter in the short time after the accident, I could definitely tell he was one that was truly loved by the city. Maybe his spirit was watching over me today. I mean, we were both from the D, so you never know. God may have indeed made a supernatural connection in the very moment my life looked like it should've been taken from me. I arrived at the hospital in about ten minutes and waited in the ER for about an hour.

"Mr. Atteley," a nurse barreled out. *Finally,* I thought. It seemed like I had been waiting for eternity. Military hospitals were no different than civilian joints, I tell you. The doc got me in the back room, moving around my arm. She was bending it and twisting it in every which way.

"Well, sir, it looks like nothing is broken, but we'll x-ray you to make sure everything is good to go." I was tired, beat and I wanted to go home. I had informed my boss on the way to the hospital that I had been in an accident. I had tomorrow off to rest up, courtesy of him, so I was gravy on that end. I took my x-rays and waited back in the ER for about another hour. I sat and twiddled on my phone, playing the few games that I did have on it. These phones sucked, though. I was missing the Sprints, Verizon's and AT&T's of the world. I was stuck with this IT&E trash truck juice. Oh well, I thought. I just had to make due with this for two years.

"Mr. Atteley?" I got up and walked back to a different doctor. As I was informed earlier, nothing was broken. I did, however, have a contusion of my left wrist and a lot of swelling. I was prescribed some Motrin for pain and given a removable wrist cast to wear for a couple of weeks. As I was given my discharge papers, my phone rang. It was Tony.

"Sup bruh?"

"A man, what the doctors say?"

"I got a wrist contusion. Got me in a removable cast for a few weeks, but I should be good.

"Good brother, good. Look, I got your rental car all set up and I'll be at the front gate in about ten minutes. Meet me outside of it." Funny we had this convo, but I still wasn't believing it. It was like it was too good to be true. I made the long walk to the gate. It really wasn't long, but when you are tired and worn out, everything seems longer and more drawn out. As I exited the main gate of the hospital, I seen a car whip around from across the street.

"Jump on in man!!!," Tony yelled. I couldn't believe it. *Thank you God,* I thought. This dude had really come through for me when I needed it most. We chopped it up as we headed to the body shop where my car was. I found out dude was a local Chamorro, but he spent most of his life growing up in L.A. We got to this body shop in the cut of the island. I swear it looked like we had driven down the road to nowhere. There were barely any street lights or any signs of life. As we got out, we were met by a lil Asian man. He was about 5'6, which was taller than most Asian men I had encountered. Mr. Lee was his name to be exact. Tony used his connections to get the accident report, which had the driver of the Ford at fault. His insurance was going to pay for my car so I was gravy.

"Here you go, sir. A Nissan Altima," said Mr. Lee. This wasn't a bad choice of vehicle to be driving temporarily until my baby got fixed up or totaled out by my insurance company. I thanked Mr. Lee and Tony for the gratitude, and was fully appreciative of everything they had done.

"Hey man," Tony said. "My sister is having a get together at a nightspot out here tomorrow night. Why don't you come through? I'll introduce you to a lot of good people." This was gravy, I thought. I could have me a cool down to take my mind off what had happened today. I told Tony to give me a call tomorrow night when he was ready and I'd roll out that way. I pulled out of Mr. Lee's Body Shop and headed towards the crib. It was now almost 8 o'clock at night, and my bed was calling me heavily. Before I got to the crib though, I stopped at Pizza Hut. A large sausage and mushroom pizza would do me right for the night, as I could stuff my fat face and just chillax with the TV on until it started to watch me. I finally got to the house and plopped on the couch. My curtain was wide open and the moon was brighter than normal. I sat there for a minute in the darkness of my confines, looking out into the world. It could have ended all today. With the impact and damage done, I should have been dead. Maybe this was a wake up call from God. Maybe it was just bad luck. I really didn't know. What I did know was that I was still alive and ticking.

I still had another moment to live out my dreams and make them into reality. Too often we don't appreciate life until we go through some life altering shit that changes our whole perspective of it. That's what I went through on this day. I didn't even cut the TV on. I simply moved myself over to one of my chairs by the window, moved the pizza box to the other one and I sat there by the window, eating in the presence of the moonlight. Food tastes different when you're going through some mental shit. It seems like the flavor is ten times better than usual. This pizza really brought me some calm. As I got down to the last slice, I stared at it. The last bite was always the best of any meal. Maybe this last bite represented the last time I would take life for granted. I folded that last piece up and devoured it.

After a hot shower and a good brush of the teeth, I plopped in my bed. Some smooth R&B blared in my headphones until I eventually drifted off into dream world. Then, not even five minutes after I took off my headphones, my phone rang. It was Kamilah, and she was in tears. We talked for the next five hours, giving each other comfort. Man, why couldn't she stay?

Friday came along faster than I had imagined. It seemed like I had just fallen asleep, then boom, it had arrived. Here it was, a day after one of the scariest moments of my life, and I didn't have any reminders except for a hurt wrist. I had the day off and I was gonna truly make it mines. It's funny how little things like the sun, which we all usually take for granted, becomes one of the most beautiful things you ever see. I may have missed my sunrise, but I definitely was grateful yesterday evening wasn't my sunset. I got up in the kitchen and started to smoke up the crack house, cooking up a dose of those GAINZ for breakfast. Corned beef hash, a shrimp and cheese omelet, and some thick ass grits. It was early, like hella early, 6:27 a.m. to be exact. I was fully awake though, and once I'm up, I'm up. I smashed that big ass plate of protein and decided to hit the pool.

I glanced off in my bathroom mirror at my 206 pound athletic build. Yea, I was a little conceited. A nigga looked hella good. I threw on my shorts, grabbed a towel and made my way down to the first floor. The parking lot was empty outside, seeing that the rest of the world was at their gigs, trying to make things happen. I strolled out the back way with confidence, stopping only to admire the beautiful trees and God crafted scenery that lined the walkway headed towards the pool and grills. As soon as I turned the corner though, I was immediately stopped in my tracks. There it was. A big ass monitor lizard, chillin' right by the gate where you entered the pool.

"YOU GOT IT MY NIGGA!!!," I shouted, as if a damn animal could understand me. Even though I know he couldn't, I sure as hell wasn't about to try and fight this battle. I had seen enough episodes of National Geographic and When Animals Attack to know that Mother Nature is not to be fucked with. My skin wasn't pale and I was not to be the next victim on one of those shows. I swear white people always got a knack for fucking with animals, and it never gets them anywhere but the ER. I know damn well y'all remember that deer who stood up on two legs and whooped that hunter's ass, with his wife of all people filming it. I hope he divorced her cause I damn sure would have. I got back to the house just in time as my phone was ringing. I peeped the screen and saw that it was Kamilah.

Me: "Sup Boo?"

Kamilah: "So I'm boo now? Boo status is reserved for my man. You doing anything tonight?"

Me: "Yea………I'm kinda hangin' out with the homies tonight, so maybe some other time."

Kamilah: "Oh…..okay."

We chopped it up a little bit more after that, but I can tell she was disappointed. I mean, she really dug me, and she was about to leave, but I wasn't giving her any time of day. In one sense, I felt bad as hell because I felt like I was treating her like a fish out of water. I was hanging the bait above her home, but just out of her reach so every time she jumped, she couldn't get it. I could only hope that I wouldn't regret it later on down the line. I quickly decided to hit the gym and crank out a hellacious leg day, seeing that I couldn't lift too much because of my wrist. I got to the car and cranked up some Freddie Gibbs. I swear that boy was a beast who was well under the radar. He had put Gary, Indiana on the map something serious when it came to rap.

Cruisin' towards Naval Base down Route 1, there I was. I found myself passing the same spot where my life seemed like it was revamped in the blink of an eye. Flashbacks played in my mind as I kept heading South past Chamorro Village, where the whole island met on Wednesday nights for food, fun and the chance to hold big ass coconut crabs. I was trying to put it behind me quickly as I had done with everything in my life. It was my way of coping and getting on with things. Up until now, the only thing I had ever lingered on was my grandmother's death. It was four months of agony and depression which saw me become a mere shell of myself. I knew that wasn't what she wanted, but it's truly hard when you lose your best friend and your whole heart. I now sat at the light, waiting for it to turn green. I saw that I was the only one at the light, which was strange for this time of the day. I looked around and noticed a man on a bike. He was dressed in all black, riding by slow. It was like a repeat of me being in the D before my cousin Eddie died. Just like that kid back home, he looked at me for a good while before he sped off. The shit was too eerie for me and I hauled ass through the light as soon as it turned green. My focus was to lift and come home in one piece. I needed to clear my mind, as reminders of my past were starting to haunt me.

I found myself working out for two hours before heading back to the crib. As I got close to the house, something told me to stop at Java Hut, the coffee shop that Kamilah brought me to when I first got here. I walked in, recognizing Ruby instantly.

"Hey there Lamar," she said with a smile while cleaning behind the counter.

"Hi," as I sat down at the counter.

"Ummm…….can I get your favorite thing on the menu?" She immediately stopped wiping.

"What's wrong? I hear it in your voice." I looked around to check for any souls in here besides mine. I knew no one was in here but me, but it took me a quick second or two for me to get myself together.

"Ruby….I'm usually the type of person who lets things go and gets over them quickly. Right now though, I feel my life kind of falling apart. I was in a car accident yesterday. Kamilah wants to be with me, but I'm not sure if I can commit to her. Haunting incidents from my hometown are eating at me. I just need some advice on what to do." She poured me a glass of water and handed it to me.

"Thank you."

"Hold on Lamar." She went to the kitchen in the back. Several minutes went by while I just sat there. I took the opportunity to really glance around the shop. It truly looked like a homegrown Starbucks. A section with leather couches, a huge bookshelf with magazines, and other good reads. As I turned over my left shoulder, there it was. It was a huge sign. "Open Mic Friday Nights." Usually, this didn't matter to me, but the way I was feeling, I needed an outlet that would be constructive. While I was going through my own struggle, I wanted to help others so they could know that their pain was felt as well. I thought about the Def Jam shows I caught at random when I was back in the states. That's when it hit me. I'll write when I get home and let my creative expression flow freely tonight. It was still gonna be on with Tony, but I had to do this for me.

"Here you go Lamar." Ruby came out from the back with two plates.

"What's this?," I said with a chuckle.

"It's a tuna panini and a spinach wrap. It's my favorite meal to indulge on when I'm in here." I took my first bite into the wrap. It was damn good. Ham, cheese and eggs wrapped in tasty goodness. I took my bite into the tuna panini. **YOWZERS!!!** The tuna tasted fresh out of the ocean. Oh yea, I could definitely fucks with this. As I continued to eat, Ruby became a friend that I needed.

"I've been here almost my whole life. I spent some time in the states. Vegas to be exact. Your town. I came back here, though. There were a lot of things that I went through personally. Adjusting to a whole new world, and coming back to a world I had known for most of my life. You're in a good position here, and having someone to look out for you is rare. Kamilah is a good person and you two need each other. She went through a lot before you came here. There she was. Sitting in the exact same seat that you are in right now, telling me her life story and all the pain she endured. I am gonna tell you like I told her. Use this place to put the worst behind you. You have a new beginning and I suggest you take advantage of it, the same way I took advantage of it when I left and came back."

I was listening loud and clear, and also indulging gratefully in this food.

"But Ruby.........I wanna live life before I settle down. I wanna be precise that all the wild stuff is out of my system. I don't wanna just mess her or any woman over." Ruby gave me a stern look as to say negro please.

"No," she said. "Be real. You wanna grip a lot of the girls on this island, get wild and then think about it when you get tired of it." She saw right through me. Why did I even try to fool an old head? More so, why did I try to fool a woman who had more than likely seen it all? Judging by the huge Mount Everest sized boulder on her finger, I should've known that a man wouldn't purchase something like that unless she was a complete woman.

"What do I do then Ruby? I mean…you tell me." With a swig of her bottled water, she uttered four words that would forever stick with me.

"You be a man." I just kept eating as she went to the back once again. I sat there and pondered what I had just heard. The life, the accomplishments, making it out of Detroit, all that was fine and dandy, however, when you are a man, you make decisions that will better you. I was bullshittin' and playin' around. I knew this deep down, but that second voice was telling me something else. As I finished up my meal, I took another look at that open mic poster.

"RUBY!! I'LL BE HERE TONIGHT," as I got to the door.

"ALRIGHT LAMAR! SEE YOU THEN! OH BY THE WAY!" She walked out and peeked her head outside of the kitchen doors. "Kamilah leaves tomorrow morning. Make a decision like a man. The mic or her?" My whole world dropped. I expected her to be here another two weeks. This shit truly caught me off guard. I had to vent something, but I wanted to see her too. She didn't call and tell me and I could understand why. I jumped in the whip and headed back to the crib.

After a fire ass shower, my bed and I became acquainted once again as I set the alarm clock for 5:15. I looked at my phone and scrolled to her number.

"I'm gone see you tonight girl," I told myself. I closed that bitch up and went back to thinking about my poetic gracefulness. I would become Def Jam tonight. I think?

I woke up early, around 4:40. I looked at my phone to see if Kamilah had texted or called me. Nothing. This girl more than likely hated me now. It was a hard pill to swallow. It was even harder to look at her like I did some of those Vegas chicks back in my day. I swear back there it was some dumb ass broads. Chalk that up to the hot ass heat or just luck of the draw. As a young cat, though, who wouldn't take advantage of a dummy, especially one with a vagina. I had this one chick that grew up like 30 miles outside of the Chi. She moved out to Vegas like a million other people. We eventually befriended each other and got sexual. Man, I smashed her on a regular and made her think we were an actual item. This girl could call me 100 times and I wouldn't answer. I would either be laid up with another chick, with the fellas, or just not feeling like talking to her. The minute I called her back, she talked to me like I hadn't ignored her a million times. This went on for years, even as I was in other relationships. I had her number blocked and unblocked at my will. It was one of those rare occurrences where as a young playa you said, this is too good to be true.

Now, those days were gone. I was a grown man. No man my age should still wanna be on that playa type bullshit. This was the time we should have things figured out, at least most of it. It was time to settle down, raise a family, and be with someone who was gonna stick with you through the long haul. I was thinking this, but also playing tug of war. I knew what I had to do. I just didn't wanna do it. Sitting on the edge of the bed, I immediately started to think about my upbringing. What I had seen as a definition of "love" in my household. As I pondered on this, it was sad that there wasn't one example of love that I had ever seen my parents exhibit. I never seen my mom and dad hold hands. I never seen them tell each other that they loved each other. I seen them kiss, but I swear that it looked like they forced that upon each other. Come to think about it, when I would go home to visit on occasion, a lot of the times, they slept in separate beds. So when did this man ever see a vision of love to copy in his own home? Never was the answer to that. It's sad too, considering that a lot of my close homies I grew up with had parents that genuinely loved each other and were happy. Joanne and Sam. Clovis and James. The Davidson's. That shit ain't easy on a kid I tell you. Seeing everyone else have a house full of love, and your house having nothing but tension, heartbreak, anger, deceit and abuse. It was enough to break you down to the lowest point you could ever imagine.

There was no reason for me to worry about ever going to hell on Judgement Day. I had lived in hell for over 18+ years in a three bedroom house on the East Side of the D. It was blue like the beautiful sky God had created, but red inside like the fire he scorched souls with as well. I grabbed my chest in that instance, thinkin' back to the day that my life changed forever. I never been shot, but it felt like the closest thing to it. Things hadn't been the same since. I thought about my sister saying she hated me, because I was loved more and favored over her. I thought about how I was once asked why I couldn't be like my best friend. Yes, I used to inhale every bit of food I seen, but why would a parent tell their child that? I am damn near thirty years old, and that shit still stings me to this day. Everyday when I work out, getting those GAINZ, I think about those words. Anger builds up inside of me. The ticking time bomb goes off and I sweat out every ounce of doubt, uncertainty and hell that I ever went through. Then, I look at myself in the mirror and wonder will I ever be asked to be like someone else again.

See, hell sometimes isn't fire with an ugly man holding a pitchfork like he was the Honorable Chairman of the Board Larry Hoover. Hell is sometimes four walls that can scream out every story that you ever been through. I stayed stuck in this position on the bed, flashbacks going through my dome faster than a cheetah chasing down a gazelle on the African Safari. Tears began to flow down my face. I had so many demons that I needed to let go of, but it was more than difficult. They say you can always forgive, but never forget. That was indeed true. However, with myself, I had to question whether I really forgave anyone truly. People make mistakes, and I know that life is a constant cycle of forgiveness, but some things shouldn't be done period. One period in my life stood out more than anything.

There I was, eighteen years old, sitting in the park by my lonesome. I had dibbled and dabbled with smoking a few times in high school, but it was never something that I ever truly enjoyed. Drinking was a different thing, as Hennessy was a girl I could always fuck with. Smoking though, nah. There I was, on a park bench, freakin' a black and mild. You know the shit feels smoother when you do that. I took my time. Occasionally I would look up and see people walking by doing their own thing. Folks in groups on the other side of the park, mobbed up talking about whatever. As I was putting the tobacco back in, all my anger and strife that I had growing up because of my household situation started to creep into my emotional cavity. I graduated school, did everything that I was supposed to do, but I felt like I hadn't did it on my own terms. Actually, besides my grandmother, Uncle James, my Aunt Anne and Aunt April, I felt like no one else had even cared. How could The Good Lord put me through shit like that? I pulled out my lighter after I was done packing that 'bacco back in. I put the black to my lips, lit it up and inhaled. It wasn't weed, but at the time, it had felt just as refreshing. As I blew out my first smoke cloud, I whispered, "God, I don't need you in my life anymore." Basically, in simple terms, I told him **FUCK YOU!** Yes, I told the Man who sent His Son to die on the cross for me, **FUCK YOU!** I told the Man who gave me the breath in my lungs, **FUCK YOU!** I told the Man who had me placed in a city where you had no choice to be tough, **FUCK YOU!**

They called us Bad Boys around here, symbolic of those 80's Pistons who used to fuck muthafuckas up on the court, including Jordan ol' milk dud head ass. I was that Bad Boy now, cause you had to be a bad muthafucka to tell God to stay the hell out of your life. That was on a Friday. I blazed that whole black, tossed it and went back to the crib. I called up a couple of homies that night to head out to one of the 18 and up spots in the city. Man we partied like tomorrow didn't exist. Nitro was the name of the joint, and much like the name, it was flaming. Girls were juking in ever direction you could imagine. Hell, me and one of my partnas were even competing to see who could get the most jukes.

"I got 43 to your 40 nigga," I told O'Bryan when we were headed back to the crib.

"NIGGA YOU DANCED WITH A FEW FAT BITCHES! THAT SHIT DON'T COUNT!" He fired that back at me real quick. I ain't care what he said. I had won, however, he was right. I did dance with a couple of round pounders that night. I was feeling good, and for the first time in my life, I had given a fat woman some attention.

I got home that night and went to sleep feeling like a new man. To not have God in your life wasn't that bad at all. I had free reign to do whatever I wanted, when I wanted. I had really thought to myself: *Why did I spend all these years showing love to an imaginary man in the sky? Fuck that shit,* I thought. I woke up Saturday still in a good mood. Moms was actually happy on that morning, as she was cooking up some cheese eggs, grits, bacon and biscuits. She knew to make my batch of bacon a lil bit on the crispy side though. I liked my shit damn near burnt. I ate up good that morning, sitting in my room, watching Saturday morning cartoons on Cartoon Network. I think that's the only thing that made me mad that morning. Coming up in the shorty years, you couldn't wait to get up at 6 or 7 in the morning. Saturday morning cartoons came on ABC, and missing them was not an option. Now those were gone, and in their place were these washed down cartoons of the 2000's, or the whack generation as I called it. Unlike the old sitcoms of the 90's like Sister Sister, Fresh Prince, Family Matters and Martin, they just didn't have that appeal. I swear if a kid ever came to me and said that their new generation was better than mine,

I know I would turn into Old Otis from Martin and beat their ass with a nightstick. I scraped the plate of that food and jumped in my whip headed towards Greek Town. All a nigga wanted to do was enjoy his day.

This was day #2 with no God in my life and it was lovely. The sun was out, no drama was going on in my view and everything was gravy. I had music blaring out of my speakers, some old Crucial Conflict to be exact. The day was just what anyone of any age needed. After mobbing through Greek Town, and all of downtown for that matter, I hit the road to mob over to Northland to get my bowl on for a few games. I remember my cousin Eddie was the king of this. Growing up, he was damn near the best in the city, as he won title after title after title. Every time I went over my aunt's house, you would see a table full of trophies. He had 'em for bowling. If he could get a trophy for the women he had as well, there would be a house full. I got in three good games by my lonesome. It wasn't packed, seeing that this was a night time jump off for the most part. I dipped out of there and drove down by Chandler Park. Man, this spot here, nigga? This spot here! If y'all ain't never heard of the "Chandler Park After Dark" video series, y'all needed to get put on to it. Any and everything you could imagine going down in the hood went down on those DVD's. Just use your imagination.

The second to last stop on this beautiful day was Eastland Mall. This was the "nigga mall" as we called it. Broads galore would be in here. Everyone would mob here, trying to get fresh for wherever they were going, or just in general. This was the D and I loved it. The day was mine. My last stop was to Louie's for my usual ham and cheese omelet, and ya boy was straight for the night. I got home that night sometime after seven. I didn't need to go out anywhere. I was feeling myself. I had a good vibe going today and yesterday. If this is what life was like without God, hell I should've not even given him the benefit of the doubt for the last eighteen years. I ended my night watching Coming to America. I swear I could watch this shit all damn night. The whole movie was funny, but there was one part that always tickled the hell out of me more than even the classic barbershop scenes. It was when Eddie was standing on the balcony after they first got that shitty apartment in Queens.

Eddie: "Behold Semi! Life...real life. A thing that we have been denied for far too long. Good morning my neighbors!"

"HEY, FUCK YOU!"

Eddie: **"YES! YES! FUCK YOU, TOO!"**

I flipped that scene back about ten times. It put the icing on the cake for me. I drifted off to sleep after Hakeem got married and was tapping Lisa's ass for eternity. One day I'll find a chick to do that with. The only thing is that I wanted me a Patrice, not no damn Lisa. I need a freak, not a good ol' girl who was scared to suck something. Sunday came around and I woke up like usual. I was brushing my teeth using that good ol' $0.79 AIM toothpaste. As I was getting my pearly whites even whiter, I looked up in the mirror. That's all I did. I looked up in the mirror. Something was different. My face was exactly the same. The same scar was on my right cheek from when I fell on my grandmother's gate when I was four.

The same scars left from when I had the chicken pox at nine were there. Two lil dots on the side of my nose and two above my eyes. Lastly, there was the scar above my right eye, which I got when O'Bryan gave me a Macho Man flying elbow during a basketball game when I was 16. My face was the same, but I felt like I wasn't looking at my own reflection. It was like an empty shell looking back at me. I brushed it off, thinking that I needed some more sleep. I returned to my bedroom afterwards to catch maybe an hour or so more of shut eye. My eyes were closed, but I didn't feel comfortable. This bed had felt like the best thing ever the last two days. Now, the mattress all of a sudden felt like I was sleeping on a bed of nails. I took this internal pain for about 30 minutes before I couldn't even take it anymore. I got up, thinking that a good batch of breakfast could make me feel better. Maybe I was getting sick and didn't know it. I really didn't know.

I went into the kitchen and poured me a bowl of Frosted Flakes. I had been smashing this since I was in diapers almost, so I know I would be straight. To my surprise, though, it did me no good. The sugar wasn't hitting, the flakes didn't feel crunchy, none of that. I knew it was fresh cause moms had just bought it and she put all the cereal in airtight containers. This was odd. Something was wrong and I didn't know what the hell it was. I calmly got up from the kitchen table and walked outside. The sun was beaming all over, but right above the house, there was a lone cloud, providing a little overcast. It just sat there. It didn't travel like the clouds usually did. It just sat there, hovering over my crib. That's when it hit me. God was indeed showing me what it was like when I had taken Him out of my life. Much like the three days it took for Jesus to rise from the dead, it took three days for me to die. This was my crucifixion. I had no cross, no nails, nor did I have a crown of thorns on my head. However, I was in more pain than ever internally. Not a physical pain, but a spiritual and emotional one. I walked back in the crib and proceeded around the house. No one was here. It was just me by my lonesome. I really felt alone. As I came back around to the living room, I glanced at the Footprints picture that my moms had hanging above the fireplace. Immediately I began to cry. That man who was being carried, I felt like that was me. I dropped to my knees, drowning my parents carpet with my sorrows.

"I'M SORRY!!! I'M SORRY GOD!!!" I yelled that over and over until I damn near went hoarse. Who was I kidding? I needed the Lord in my life much like we all did. I begged and pleaded for forgiveness. By the time I looked up, two hours had passed by. I don't know if that was enough to have God forgive me, but I certainly had hoped it did the job. Obviously He did, though, seeing the position that my life was in now.

It was now 5:30. I was gone drive down to Java Hut, but what the hell, I thought. It was only maybe a ten minute walk by foot and the sun was out shining bright as ever. I started the trek down the long, gravel entrance way that led to my condo complex. Off to the left, the Sheraton looked like a giant lego monstrosity of a building. I hadn't been up in there since I got here, so I would definitely have to roll that joint up one of these days. As I got to the main road, I noticed more than the usual. It was one thing to drive this everyday, but walking, it looked totally different. They called this street out here "Stab Row." Trust, it didn't look nothing like the blocks back home, but, from the times I drove down this way at night, I could tell you that there was very little lighting. If you did wanna mess somebody up, then this was the perfect place to do it. Not to mention that the police force on Guam was small to death, so it would take a good while for them to get to the scene of a crime. I made it to the end of the block with no problem. Wasn't no waiting for the light to turn green. I did the American thing. I waited for the coast to be clear and ran my tail across the street. As the coffee shop came into view, I could see that a nice crowd was already gathered inside. Approaching even closer, I came to the conclusion that whoever was on the mic needed to stop singing. I understand that they had a guitar and was doing a cover of someone else, but if you can't sing it like the original artist, or just make it sound good, then you shouldn't be singing. I entered at the midpoint of the song, taking a seat at the first table next to the door. I was the only brother in here. It was all locals and they were deeply in tune with their own. As ol' boy's performance ended, I walked up to the counter to order me that fire ass tuna panini that Ruby laced with crack. I also signed my name on the list, deep down hoping that I wouldn't be called.

"How about another round of applause?" The crowd followed upon Ruby's request. This was cool, though, seeing that there was something out here to keep the community vibing at peace. I mean, I hadn't heard anything negative about Guam. Even so, it was still good to see something so positive. If only my hometown could be this good.

"Now everybody, for a different feel. I met this guy a few weeks back." That's all I heard as I was saying in my head, *'please don't call me.'* I really was totally oblivious to what Ruby was saying, as that phrase kept echoing in my head.

"Give it up for Lamar!!" There was an applause, but one that basically said, who in the good hell was this guy?? I nervously got up and walked over towards the stage. I hadn't felt this queasy since my homey asked me to stash a pistol in my backpack way back in the 7th grade. I got on stage more nervous than the chicken who crossed the road because he saw two niggas.

"Hello everyone?" I got about three hi's from the crowd. The rest had me nervous. I knew deep down it was because I wasn't Chamorro. I was basically the odd ball out in the room. *Fuck it*, I thought. I had to go for mine.

"I'm originally from Detroit, Michigan and I have never done this in my life. So I'm gonna recite the only piece I ever memorized, and that is one of a great poet I know named Deacon Blair." God honestly, it was the only piece I had memorized. Truthfully, I didn't know a Deacon Blair. I had just heard his stuff one night when I was with a homegirl at a spotlight show while visiting L.A. I dug that joint, even though I wasn't a fan of the art. I was just trying to be in her good vibes so she would let me tax that ass. Oh yea, it happened too. I had written my own piece, memorized it, but I was scared shitless that I would screw up. Then, at the last second, I said fuck it. If I fuck up, I fuck up. Finally, I let the words roll off my tongue and left it all on that makeshift stage.

INTERNALIZE

I used to be an open door, allowing people to enter into
my home freely,
experiencing my hospitality, feeding them my food,
watching my television, letting them sit in my chairs, and the
reaction I got were stares
Why is this here, why is this there, why do you have two
levels instead of three
See, I used to be an open door, very accepting of
strangers, that's until I found out danger comes in the form
of being yourself; they tell you be you, but hate me when I'm
me, so I change the lock and key, only allowing access to
those in my small circle
I literally went from external to internal, no longer open
as I once was, I don't beg for hugs, I don't beg for
acceptance, I embrace resistance, my persistence in my
growth has shown in more ways than one, so why shall I
become one that everyone else wants
This is why I separate and dissected former friendships
and kinships and got into a partnership with my
penmanship, to express myself when no one wanted to listen,
when no one wanted to understand
So I stand a man on my own two, decreasing myself
around those who love to put on shows and increasing myself
around those who just want uncut television without
interruption
See, change is nothing more than loose metal, but dollars
don't fold unless others apply pressure, and love of money is
the root of all evil, so let 'em love me to hate me
because I'd rather be hated for being loose

than loved for being able to fold

"Thank You"

There was about three to four seconds of silence. I didn't know what to expect. You could hear a rat piss on cotton and a roach take a breath inside the wall. All of a sudden a huge roar came out. They were actually feeling me. Holy shit! I couldn't believe it. I walked back to my seat, high fivin' folks and saying thank you's while soaking up the compliments along the way. As another guy got up to continue to host, Ruby joined me at the table.

"Here Lamar. You deserve this. Good job."

"Thanks Ruby," I said excitedly, as my stomach was rumbling graciously at the sight of this tuna panini. We sat and talked for damn near the next two hours as we indulged in different acts of music, singing and poetry. My eyes were starting to open up to another way of life. I was starting to see the world for what it was, a beautiful place. We watch the news media of the world and see nothing but death and destruction. Wars in The Middle East. Countries going broke and not being able to feed their people. Young black teens getting gunned down by neighborhood watch captains and watching them walk away scott-free because of the Amerikkkan UN-justice system. That was the world we, including myself, viewed on a daily. This, however, was showing me a totally different avenue. Long gone was the mindset of a neighborhood kid living off Warren and Chalmers. What had arrived was the thinking of a king who was preppin' to sit on his throne. This was the start. My finish would be when I was buried six feet, locked in a casket, in a black suit, hiding the bullet wounds that would take me out. Only the greats died at the hands of assassin's bullets.

6 NEW YEAR, NEW PAIN

The time was passing by faster than a running back on the Indianapolis Colts porous run defense. Kamilah was gone and I had fucked up by not seeing her the night before she left. I chose Tony over her, and I highly regretted it. On the other hand, things were on the up and up. In a little bit under eight months, I had received a promotion at my government job to head intel analyst. I was connected beyond belief with people from all over.

Lastly, I took my black ass to the Philippines. It was ten days of madness. I was sent up with a crew of guys from work to meet with Philippine intel analysts. Our job was to train them up in the latest technologies involving cyber defense and discuss ways that we could improve our cyber security over the long haul. Work was work, and we did our job as we were paid to do. However, when the time came to play, we played hard. The first night was spent doing some of everything. Me, my main assistant Eric, and a super tall light skinned brother named Tony, a top notch computer programmer. We headed out into Olongapo City to get a kick out of the night life. A U.S. Navy ship was also moored here for a port visit so the term "turnt up" was an understatement. We hit The Barrio, a strip of road laced with "clubs." This was nothing more than a district where any and everything was legal. My guys were on one, but I kind of played in the background, soaking in the sights around me, analyzing the lifestyles that I seen before me. As we walked up the streets, camcorder in Eric's hand, we were stopped by a group of young children. They had to be no more than five or six, but they were begging for money and trying to sell us some fried pork skins. Now I rocked with the swine, but my mind was kind of twisted. Here are five or six year olds out in the streets after the sun went down, trying to scrape up money to do whatever. Now I was a bullshitter coming up so I knew bullshit when I seen it, but, I knew these kids really were trying to live. There were grown Filipino adults riding through the streets on bikes, not even giving two looks to these children. It was plain as day. These kids were tasked to bring back money from the foreigners to help feed whoever was in the household. I couldn't even imagine the horror they were feeling. It may look like nothing to us, but to see a kid in this position bothered me some. How can you be a kid when you don't even have a chance to be a kid? As we continued on, we made it to the end of the strip.

"This it. Y'all wanna get it up in here?," Tony clamored.

"Let's roll," I said. Eric followed along as we went into EMU. That was the name. Upon entering, there was a lady at the desk with a younger looking lady. Immediately the hustle was on as she was trying to persuade us to buy girls for a good time. She escorted us inside where my lessons of learning this wild country continued. At first sight there was a stage full of young Filipino women. The club was semi packed and all around, these squids from the states were locking up everything they seen. I may have never been in the Navy, but one thing I did know about sailors was that they don't hesitate to pay for some pussy. It's what they do.

"You sit here. Sit here." Mamasan, as I called her, put us on a plush couch behind a table in view of the whole joint.

"Drinks gentlemen?"

"Hennessy!," I blurted out. I may have been analyzing, but I wasn't gonna turn down my medicine.

"Hennessy for all of us," Eric followed. Me and Tony looked at him and just stared. He may have been quiet as a mouse, but when it came to getting his drink on, if one was drinking, we all were gonna drink. Some young ladies joined us at the table making conversation and getting their laugh on.

"Here, more drink." Mamasan came back with two more glasses for everyone.

"We ain't order anymore drinks," I told her.

"I know. Sailors pay." She pointed over to a group of men. We looked over and they just started hollerin' and raising their bottles in the air. One of them had on a TMT shirt for Mayweather. I swear I wished Pacquiao would quit being scared and get his ass whipped already. Who knows, maybe it would happen and then he would come up with some excuse as to why he lost, such as a shoulder injury. The club was full of women and my buzz was starting to kick in something serious. By this time, I had about five Henn dogs and had been getting rubbed on, kissed on, all that. Tony had drifted upstairs to the hotel portion where he was more than likely knocking some chick's lung out of place with the mighty black snake.

I had Eric's camcorder as I was filming everything I was seeing, all while getting felt up. I wasn't giving this chick a damn thing, but I did enjoy it much. What I caught on camera was beyond wild. The women were now completely naked, entertaining everyone in here. In one corner, head was being given. In another section, there was a live sex show on the couch while others sat right next to em, continuing to drink like nothing was happening. As for me, I was zoned the hell out. Baby girl had left me now, seeing that she wasn't getting anything out of me. Meanwhile, Eric was selling this chick in all yellow a dream.

"I'm gonna marry you, bring you back to the states and you will have my babies." I knew this nigga was beyond drunk, but damn. He told her ass he was gonna marry her. You can't fool around like that out here. As many brothers I seen with Filipino wives in the states, I couldn't even play like that. We got it in for hours until we finally were stumbling back to our hotel somewhere in this city. As I laid in bed that night, well past three in the morning, I was grateful that we weren't meeting up with the analysts, that way I could rest up something serious. On the other hand, the liquor was wearing off and my upbringing was kicking back in. As much fun as I had, it just wasn't right. Young girls selling themselves out for an old retired military geezer who ran the nightspot. Kids begging for money. No fucks were given. This wasn't me anymore. That night, that first one out of ten, showed me how much I had grown. Yes I had truly become a man, because a man doesn't enjoy things like that.

I didn't want to go to hell when I took my final breath. However, I didn't have to worry about that, seeing that I was visiting hell. That hell was called Subic Bay. That hell was called Olongapo City. That hell is what I pray my daughter would never have to experience in her life.

HELL

I recently walked thru hell, watchin' women cast under a
devil's spell where they dispelled their bodies for dollas.
I watched men play devil's advocate, payin' for slayin'
sessions to achieve a quick high, only to say goodbye and
leave her for the next man to occupy.
I saw this vision all throughout hell, except this hell
wasn't filled with fire and brimstone; instead, it had flashing
lights and neon signs, beggars and bare foot children
watchin' mommy from outside, not knowin' what's goin' on
inside,
or what's goin' inside of her, and to my dismay, I played
the game as well, droppin' dollas from the sky, not realizing
the kickin' and scratchin' that occurred for one dead face,
seein' their faces light up because here in this hell, this dolla
was more than enough to keep the lights on in their own
homes,
and as I got to my temporary home, I finally realized the
consequences of my actions and they showed lack of
compassion, cause what was occurring was modern day
trappin'.
Nothin' to do with the white and green exchanging
hands, but money and sex going hand in hand, interlocked

as panties dropped for the pain of pleasuring a dick for what
in America wasn't the price of a nick bag.
If they got lucky, they got the price of a dime bag: this
was drugs of another level. See, this was the devil's
playground, and here, the minds of innocence was played so
they could be manipulated to portray the sex trade in an
undercover status.
Here it wasn't 'bout what chick was the baddest, but who
could set that ass out the fastest,
cause as soon as the door swung open, legs opened for the
highest bidder, and if the price was right, the wheel would be
spinning several times until it was time to go,
and tomorrow, the cycle would continue itself all over
again. Some people call this hell, I simply call it.....
The Philippines.

New Year's Eve 2012 was here. I had my tix to the big
bash at the Sheraton across from my house. All the partners
from work and the Air Force base in general were gonna be
there. I had already laid out my game plan. I was leaving all
my keys in the house minus the house key. I would walk to
the hotel but stumble back to the house.

Knock, Knock, Knock. I cracked open the door to see
who this was disturbing me on my vacation.

"Bestie, what's good?!" It was my homegirl Lhea. I met
her at the barbershop like two months after I got here. The
homies at work had plugged me with this cat named Joe who
was a monster with the clippers. That was my biggest
concern when I got here. Unlike white folks, brothers just
don't let anyone slice em up. You mess up our cut and we're
pissed off for a few weeks. You mess up our lining and we

liable to take a life. 'Salon Fusion' was the name of the joint. It was located in the Agana section of the island, right inside their watered down version of a mall.

"Sup F.O.L.K.S.?" I was greeted by a barber who looked like he was fresh out the joint.

"Sup my nigga?," I replied. Yea, this dude wasn't just over here for some island life. He had golds in his mouth and a big ass six point star tattooed on his neck. Wherever he was from, he was definitely 7-4 to the fullest.

"BOLO my nigga."

"Lamar," as I dapped him up.

"You looking for Joe right? He ran inside the mall for a quick bite real quick. Just gone head and wait in the chair. He said you were coming. So how you enjoyin' the island?" That deep breath came out before anything.

"Man, I'm maintaining. Still getting used to everything. So where you from my dude? I see you 6 riding."

"Mississippi my nigga," responding to me as he kept focus on giving the cat in the chair a sick edge up with the razor. "Came out here to get free from some shit at the crib. It ain't the best thing in the world, but it beats taking the risk of sitting in a cell ya feel me."

I wasn't too keen on niggas who dropped their billy bad ass stories upon first meeting them. His demeanor however and the tone of his voice let me know he was serious and not trying to impress me. I could respect that.

"What's up man? You Lamar?" I turned around in the chair to see this light skinned Pretty Ricky type nigga. Nigga looked like Klay Thompson from the Warriors.

"Joe?"

"Yea bruh." "What you getting today?," as he draped the barber apron over me and buttoned it around my neck.

"Bald fade, mid length, wave length on top." As he started to get his clippers together, out of the back she came. She was the only sister in here and she was thick as hell. Not to mention she was fine in the face. Honestly, besides a few of those Air Force chicks, this was one of the top notch chicks I had seen on this island. As Joe began to slice me up, I kept tabs over her, making sure not to be staring though. She looked like she was upset. Maybe she was, or maybe it was just one of those days. However, shorty was fine and I definitely wanted to get to know her. A half hour passed and I was finally done.

"How's that bruh?" Joe put the mirror to my face. Oh yea, I was definitely impressed. I slid him the $20 with much respect behind it. Homeboy definitely made me feel and look good. BOLO head was out of the chair and we all went outside to smoke some blacks and just conversate. I wasn't a fan of smoking, but I indeed felt good enough to light up, bringing back one of my teenage pleasures. Lhea came outside after about five minutes and joined the convo. The boys' next two customers came in and we continued talking outside. I found out she was from Kansas City, Missouri. She was Filipino, Black and Swedish. I really didn't give a damn what she was mixed with. All I knew was that she was fine as shit.

"So what's up? You ready to get it in?," walking into my crib sporting a blue and white fit.

"Girl, I'm bout to walk over here and stumble back. This almond milk that I'm pouring up right now will be the only non alcoholic thing going into my system tonight. Gone smash some of this corned beef and cabbage on the stove so you can get something in your stomach girl." We chilled in the house smashing, laughing and watching TV, passing time by until it hit 9:30. By then, I had gotten about 10 calls from my guys telling me to hurry up because they were already there starting the party. I threw on some custom made gear I had made over here. Black and taupe was the color of the fit, with the sleeve cuffs and collar matching the material and design of the slacks. Adding some black cuff links with the chrome finish, I was definitely the freshest brother on the G tonight. Shit, I was looking slicker than a can of oil. As we made our way down the elevator and out the building, headed to the hotel, I just marveled at the stars in the clear night sky.

It was New Year's Eve, and I could actually walk down a street at night. Had I been in the D, I wouldn't even think about walking anywhere outside. Gunshots would be going off like fire alarms. Plus, living in the D, you damn sure didn't know if those bullets were going in the air or heading straight towards your dome. The stars in the sky represented to me each soul my city had lost to stupid ass violence, some of which I witnessed personally. From family to friends dying, I witnessed it all. The shit damn near wanted to make me cry, but I had to keep living my life and put the past behind me. Lastly, it popped in my head that I was celebrating New Year's overseas. Now how many of y'all can say y'all did that?

"MARRRRRRRRRRRRRRRRRRRRRR!!!!!!!" I hadn't even gotten three steps past the last step leading down to the ballroom when Puncho greeted me. I dapped my dude up. It was good to see the homey.

"And who is this lovely lady may I ask?," as he grabbed her hand and kissed it like a gentlemen.

"Why, thank you. I'm Lhea. Such a gentleman, I see."

"When someone loves you, they always think you're beautiful. Those who don't see your beauty can't really see you at all, and I love you, simply because you're woman." He kissed her hand again and this girl couldn't stop blushing. I swear this boy mouthpiece was so smooth he could talk the roots of a plant into walking away from the soil. As him and Lhea continued their conversation, I made it over to the buffet to smash on some grub before I started my drunken escapades. I hung off in the distance with my plate in hand, listening to the music blaring from the ballroom, looking at all these local women in here. Some of them were sexy, I'll give 'em that, however, a lot of them were some big girls. For the most part, most of them were built this way over here.

It was now 10:23. I was in full fledge mode now. Puncho, Lhea and a bunch of other cats I knew from work were getting it in on the dance floor. Me? I was on Hennessy #3. At this rate, I would be stumbling by 10:45. I started my drinking at 10:07 on the dot. Three drinks in 16 minutes was not what my liver wanted. It was probably starting its disintegration process right now. The music kept thumpin'. The drinks kept getting downed. Henn after Henn after Henn. Hell, I don't even remember going on the dance floor, but I found myself out there.

"ONNNNNNEEEEE MINUTEEEEEEEE!!!" The MC of the event yelled that over the mic. I hadn't even realized it was one minute until the start of 2013. I looked up at the big wall through my blurred vision and seen 11:59:23 til midnight projected on it. My head was spinning, but it was in a good way. Everything seemed to be moving slower than a turtle at this point. I had a good vibe going. I could feel my arms raise. I could feel the breath leaving my lungs as I yelled and screamed. I felt the emotion from the young lady that hugged me and gripped me as if I was her man.

"5-4-3-2-1. HAPPY NEW YEAR!!!" We all shouted loudly, grateful to see a new year. I had lost Lhea by this point, but I had this fine piece of Italian work in front of me. I slobbed her down in my drunken state and didn't regret not one bit of it. The fireworks were poppin' outside. I was lip locked with a stallion. I was living the life overseas. Who in the good hell could tell me anything right now? The answer? Not a damn person on this Earth.

I woke up the next morning hanging over my bed, with a nasty pile of vomit soaked into my carpet on the side of my joint. My head was throbbin' and spinnin'. If I could detach it from my neck and sit it on a mantle to chill for a while I would. I barely made out the time, but it was 1:29 in the afternoon. I don't remember how I got in or who was in here with me. I slowly crept up and sat on the bed. I felt like shit. I knew I wasn't going anywhere today. As I slowly waltzed my hungover self to the bathroom, I had to bust out a sonar piss. For y'all that don't know, that's when us men don't turn on any lights. You aim for where you think the toilet is. When you hear water, you keep your dick pointed in that direction until you're finished. It may have been day time, but all my curtains and blinds stayed closed to keep sunlight out, so it was darker than usual. Squinting through everything, I saw a square on my mirror. I cut on the light and you would have thought I was a gremlin. Light was my biggest enemy as it seemed to make my head pound even more. It was a sticky note.

"We brought you home. You were beyond tore up and we put you in the bed. I took ya clothes off cause you threw up on em on the way there. Don't worry, I didn't rape you. LOL. Lhea." I wanted to laugh, but I couldn't because I was so slizzard. I just balled that sheet up and waltzed it back over to the bed, crashing out once again.

I woke up a lil bit after 8 o'clock, feeling about 75% better. It wasn't where I wanted to be, but it was damn sure better than where I was at before. I was hungry as shit. I hadn't ate all day and I definitely needed a fix. I threw on a beater and some basketball shorts and headed to the whip to make my way over to KINGS for a late night meal. They knew me up in there 'cause I was damn near there every weekend. I made my way in there, with the usual folks behind the register for the late night shift. Ordering my ham, mushroom, bacon and spinach omelet, I chilled on the cushioned bench, waiting for my comfort food to come so I could head to the crib for good. The noise from outside was pestering me as it was a bunch of young Navy cats screaming and carrying on like they were nutty. How did I know they were Navy you ask? Well only sailors get drunk and talk about work. I heard ship this and ship that. When I got drunk, I just wanted to sleep.

"Mar bro, waddup?" I looked up to see one of my Chamorro homies I called "Big Red." He was from the south tip of the island called Agat. Now they had their version of the Bloods down there. I didn't and couldn't take them serious, seeing that this was Guam and there was no way in hell you could bang living in a village, on a tropical island where it was 105 degrees everyday. However, he worked out at the gym I went to so we were good. I chopped it up with him for 'bout a good minute, dapped him up and he walked off with his boys.

"Order for Lamar," the woman said from behind the counter. I thanked her as I grabbed the bag and expected this to be just a normal trip back. As I turned around though, I was in for a shock. These fools were brawling outside, rather it was Red and his homies beating the shit out of these Navy cats. I had heard that the locals got their pleasure in jumping the Navy dudes, but I just couldn't see them doing it for no reason. I rolled dolo 99.9% of the time out here and I never had a problem. I just stood there, letting out a chuckle as the "C'mon man" from one of the white boys was immediately met with a swift fist to the face. These fools were down and out for the count. 5 on 4 maybe, but something had to provoke them. I know damn well they ain't just walk out the restaurant from eating and start handing out hay makers.

"Man, what the hell Red?" I asked him, walking out with my food.

"These fools popped off at the mouth bout my people blood. I don't take that shit!!!," as he kicked one of the white dudes one last time in his stomach. All I could do was laugh at these fools.

"Y'all be easy bruh."

"You too, blood," Red responded back. Man, eating to soothe my soul was one thing. To end my night with seeing a vicious ass whooping that was well deserved, it was priceless. There are some things that money can't buy. For everything else, there's an ass whoopin'. To hell with Mastercard. Those Navy cats needed the All State man right about now. They needed to be in some good hands, cause from the looks of it, they damn sure didn't have 'em.

7 THE CHALLENGE

The New Year's shenanigans were over and it was back to regular life as normal. I was back at work, making the good money while making the tough decisions. Not to mention that I didn't have that rental anymore. The Chrysler was fixed and again in daddy's possession.

"Atteley, we need to talk." I turned around in my chair to see it was my boss Mr. Wilder.

"Aight I'm coming." Nothing out of the ordinary had happened, so I wasn't worried about anything. I got into his office and plopped down on his nice plush couch, analyzing the plaques on the wall from his 30 years of military service.

"Ok Lamar. First off, you are doing great things and you have more than met the expectations. However, down south needs some help." I had a puzzled look on my face as I really didn't know what was going on.

"What you mean boss man?" He bit into his Filipino snack and mumbled out some more nonsense.

"Basically, on the Navy side of the house, it's shit. I mean, deep shit. They need someone to train and revamp everything about their systems down there. You start next week. Same pay, same benefits. Just a whole new crowd of people that you have to deal with." I'll be hot damned, I thought. I was comfortable, settled in and basking at this job. Now, I had to go train some other mofos who couldn't get their shit together. *Ain't this bout a bitch,* I thought. I walked out the office upset. I really hated being jerked around like this, but I had to do what I had to do I guess.

I got home that evening around 5 and just chilled out on the couch. TV wasn't interesting, so I went and grabbed a huge thick notebook that I never used. I meant to use this for note taking at work, but all it did was collect dust in my closet. I put the TV on mute and just pondered on what to write. I could easily write some poetry, because it didn't take a genius to put words together. I simply wrote one word and one letter, **BANDAGES 2.** I kind of looked at the paper strange and laughed. Was I really thinking about writing a book? More so, how in the good hell could I write a **BANDAGES 2** when there wasn't even a **BANDAGES 1?** I closed up the notebook and prepped myself to jump in this shower so I could relax for the rest of the night. That's when the phone rang. It was my pops.

Me: "Sup pops?"

Pops: "Ya Granny gone."

Time stood still as I tried to ponder what my dad had just told me. I was in stunned silence.

"Lamar, you knew it was coming. I did. We all did. She was sick for a long time and those kidneys just couldn't keep up. It was her time, Mar." My dad said that simply with no emotion at all. In a normal circumstance, I would be upset, however, I knew my father. He had emotions. He just didn't show 'em. He never did and he never would. He was hurting inside, but he wasn't gonna show it.

"Pops, I start a new position in a week so I won't be able to make it."

"It's ok. Yo' granny know you loved her. I understand. We all understand. Do what you gotta do." I hung up and just broke down right there on the floor in front of my closet. Now I had no grandmothers left. Mama's mama gone. Daddy's mama gone. The worst part about this one is that I wouldn't even have the chance to tell her goodbye. She died in the hospital and that's where my last memory of her was at. I seen her when I went back home for that day and a half. It was brief, but I managed to get 30 minutes with her. We watched Maury together and she was laughing hysterically. For a woman in her 80's, she had one of the brightest spirits you could ever imagine.

What I remember vividly is that the doctors didn't wanna give her some green tea and she raised hell about it. If there was one thing that you weren't gonna keep away from my granny, it was some green tea. After a few curse words all in the name of Jesus, she finally got her 4oz. I thought it was funny as hell. At that moment, the tears broke and I cracked a smile. At least my last memory of her was a good one and not that of suffering. This added to my stresses for the day, but none the less, life had to continue.

I finished out the week with no qualms and rolled right into the weekend, needing a big pick me up. The gym session was brutal and satisfying, but I needed to get loose, feel free and live on the edge for a minute. That's when my phone rang.

Me: "Preach Puncho."

Puncho: "Meet us down on the docks in Agat at 1. Bring $100 and a bottle of whatever. We need to turn up for a good minute and rap on real nigga shit."

Me: "Aight, got you."

Puncho: "Gone."

Just when you were hoping that God was reading your mind and going to answer your prayer requests, there He came. I had time to kill. It was just 11 and the docks were nothing more than a 20 minute drive. I wanted to be symbolic today. I wanted to dress in something that represented me. I got out my blue gear for the day. A navy blue Detroit Tigers fitted with my blue and white Nike's. I always kept my watch and shades game on point. Today would be nothing less. I decided to rock the Marc Jacobs joint I copped over here and lace up my face with the Prada shades. They were on the pricey side, but this is how I did it with these two items. I heavily starched up the 'Against All Odds' tee, put the razor sharp creases in my blue jeans and a nigga was ready. I looked in my almost full body mirror to analyze myself.

I was down this week with granny dying and having to adjust to a brand new group of workers. For a few hours though, I could get a pick me up to be reminded that the world ain't over. So many times as humans, we have a hard time adjusting to the changes around us, or the ones that involve us directly. It is in those times, though, that we truly realize how much strength we have as individuals. This man right here was strong. My reflection said something different as it looked back at me like, I am that muthafucka. I am that muthafucka who survived the D. I am that muthafucka who made life great for myself in Sin City. I am that muthafucka who is now taking like by the horns and fucking it raw on a little island in the middle of the Pacific Ocean. I was that muthafucka. Lamar Atteley III. I strolled out the house like my dick was the biggest on Earth, and I was the King of Jupiter. I slid into the whip and let K. Dot take me down the freeway.

Pour up, drank, head shot, drank
Sit down, drank, stand up, drank
Pass out, drank, wake up, drank
Faded, drank, faded, drank
Now I done grew up round some people living their life in bottles/Granddaddy had the golden flask backstroke every day in Chicago...........

Chicago mane. Now that was a rough city. I had family just East of them across the border in Indiana. I definitely rocked with them and had to get back down there the first chance I got. Hollin' at one of my cousins before I left the crib, their whole city was stoked on the fact one of their own made it to the league. E'Twuan Moore was a beast in college, so I expected nothing less when he hit the big time in the NBA. It was good to see cats make it from the damn near impossible to the bright lights. Detroit had Jalen Rose, Joe Louis and Antonio Gates just to name a few. Hell, shootin' down to San Diego a few times, I remember seeing Gates in the club. Man, that damn Pretty Ricky Fontaine lookin' muthafucka would woo women with his smile. Me and some of my Vegas partnas were in club 94 some years back out there and he walked in the club. It was like all pussy had a magnet and attracted straight to his ass. I mean, he took all the hoes without even trying to take all the hoes. I was salty as shit he came in here and did this, but I couldn't be totally mad at him. We had that charm in the D. That's just how we did. We took another city's females with no hesitation.

I hit the docks right at 12:34. Gulping down this last C2 green tea, I got out the car to a sight of nothing but gorgeous women. *Oh yea,* I thought, this day was definitely going to be fun.

"My nigga, welcome." I dapped Puncho up as he greeted me, beach hat and Rajon Rondo Celtics jersey on as his cool me down gear.

"A look mane. We gone have fun today. We gone laugh, joke, chill, play with these females, all that. But most importantly, most importantly my nigga, we gone sit down and discuss ways to become better. However, the fun is first." I nodded my head up and down in agreement.

"All day my nigga. Let's do this," as I seen some more ass walk by. We had some time to spare before we loaded up on this long ass yacht, ready for things to get crackin' off. By now, the rest of the fellas had gotten down here and it looked like it was gonna be a good ass time.

"A LOOK AT THIS NIGGA DREW COMING DOWN AND SHIT LOOKIN' LIKE T.D. JAKES SON!!!" I turned around at the sight of whoever said that and burst out in laughter. My guy Drew, a.k.a. "Saxman," had come strolling down the pier in his silk button up, slacks and dress shoes. Nigga looked like he was going to preach a sermon rather than chill on a yacht.

"You casket clean ain't you bruh?," as I dapped my folks up.

"Man, I'm just trying to be like you."

"Naw man. I'm tryna be like you. Creflo ain't got shit on you mane." It was all love. It was times like this that I truly appreciated life and all that it had to offer. We had the homies, the females, drink and food. We didn't need anything else. We loaded up the yacht and took off at about 15 minutes past one. Immediately, every living soul hit the top of the boat, enjoying the outside vibe and great weather. I was stealing some of the homey, Fergie's wings that she cooked, while holding a glass of champagne. Hell, Puncho was pouring everyone a glass. We had every type of person on here, including a dude who had more sugar inside of him than a pack of Oreos. It was gravy, though. As long as he didn't bother me, I was gravy.

"A-A, y'all gather round for this toast!!!" Puncho got everybody to hold their glasses in the air.

"A LOOK, THIS SO FADED ENTERTAINMENT!!! THIS IS THE SHIT WE DO!!! WE GONE HAVE FUN, KICK IT LIKE G'S, AND WE GONE TURN THIS MUTHAFUCKA UP, OUT, AROUND AND

WHATEVER OTHER WAY Y'ALL WANNA GO!!! SO FADED!!!" The roar from everyone shook the boat as we hit glasses and gulped down our drinks. What went down for the next five hours was anything but boring. You had the token drunk white boy who passed out from just drinking too much. Girls were kissing girls. Niggas were jumping off the top of the yacht and into the ocean. I watched and applauded them 'cause my black ass wasn't about to try it. My black ass couldn't swim. I wasn't about to be fish food for no shark, stingray, whale, or whatever else was in the water. By four o'clock, everyone was just in chill mode, choppin it up as folks were trying to let some of the liquor dissipate.

"A Lamar, come join me downstairs on the inside please?" I obliged to Puncho's request as I poured me another glass of Champagne. I walked down inside this lavish vessel. I don't think any of us had even been down here for the damn near three hours we were out here on the water. The inside was something that you would only see in movies. Hardwood floors with gold chandeliers. The unused bars had marble tops, so you know they definitely got it in with this thing.

"Man, how much did this cost?," I asked him.

"There's no price on the enjoyment of life. Gone sit down man." We were at one of the booths chilled out and focused. This reminded me of the Dutch Schultz scene at the end of Hoodlum where he was sitting with another gentleman in the restaurant before he met his ultimate demise. He sipped his champagne, staring at me. I sipped back, staring at him, analyzing and trying to decipher his intentions.

"Let's rap," I told him. He folded his hands and leaned in forward.

"What does the term extraordinary gentleman mean to you?" I answered his question with another question.

"What makes you extraordinary?" He leaned back, not saying a word, eyes on me the entire time. This was like a game of chess, with two kings who didn't wanna budge and be the first one to open up. We were both in the same position. We knew of each other, but we didn't truly know each other.

"Break this down. You grow up with roaches and project buildings. You see death at every turn. You EMBODY the environment you were raised in. The next minute, you're poppin' bottles all over the world. You're having chicks dome you up at the snap of your fingers. You have money like you never seen. YOU HAVE.....excellence. And what does it cost? Tell me, what does it cost?" I sipped my champagne once again.

"Life," I whispered. Puncho nodded his head up and down.

"That's right...if you are a basic thinker. The true answer is death." Now I leaned forward.

"How you figure philosopher?" He got a chuckle out of that, as did I.

"I see you are indeed a chess player. You answer one move with another. I can respect that. However, when you move, you always leave something open. Death is how all this happens. You have to bring death to your upbringing. You have to bring death to your once shallow mindset. You must introduce death to the government traps you were encased in. There is no life without death. Imagine life just being life, not being able to end in an earthly fashion. Everyone from the first man and woman still here and you couldn't die. You would have a bunch of people suffering, tortured by their fellow man to be supreme. You wanna die, but you can't because there is no death. Death, to old things, are what brings life to extraordinary things. Things that aren't so simple. Things that are simple. Death brings that. And you, you have the greatness in you. But you must die in order to bring life to a new phase you have growing inside of you." At this time, the tension was so thick that you could cut it with a butter knife.

"You're going through something right now and I can tell. I could tell the minute you walked up that pier. Your spirit spoke to me. Now what is it?" The stare down continued. I was thinking to myself, *was this guy a Pope slash Nastradamus type negro??* I grabbed the almost empty bottle of champagne from across the table, never taking my eyes off of him. I sat there with it in my hand, staring him down as if he killed my mother and this was my chance at revenge. I downed the rest of the bottle and tossed it across the lower level we were on. The glass smashed against the wall. Puncho was unfazed.

"Look…you have a nice gift. I will give you that. You spoke to my spirit. I'll give you that, however, don't think you know me."

"I DON'T HAVE TO KNOW YOU!!!," as he slammed his hands on the table, standing up out of his seat, hovering over me. I rose up and met him face to face, hands on the table.

"Then what??" It was like two pit bulls about to fight over the last piece of meat. He closed his eyes for a minute, re-opened them and told me the realest shit alive.

"That reaction. How you just got in my face. You take that same challenge and meet it…face to face. You are

150

extraordinary, but it's for you to discover." He slowly crept away from the table and all I could do was stand there, still, silenced at what had just taken place. Right as he got to the door leading back out, he turned around.

"And remember, Lamar, sometimes extraordinary men become basic in the mind." He walked out the door and left me there to ponder his words. I sat back down in that booth undisturbed all the way until we pulled back in. When we got back, I took my time watching everyone else exit the yacht. Drew came down.

"Hey man, you good? I ain't see you upstairs for like the last two hours."

"I'm good, Drew. I just got hit with a reality check that I needed." Drew patted my shoulder and walked off to leave me by my lonesome. I slowly made my way off the yacht and to my car, not saying anything to anyone. I know Puncho meant no harm in his words, but that was the only way that I was gonna get that message. I sped off heading back to the crib. My ride home was a quiet one. No K Dot, no Cole, no Drake, no nothing. I needed to ponder my thoughts and how I was gonna go about things from this point on. Saturday was still early, and I was trying to think about something to do. I couldn't think of anything in particular until I thought about a sign I seen posted around the Air Force base. The African American Heritage Association on base was hosting a conscious open mic tonight. I knew folks up there, but I didn't know em. *Fuck it,* I thought. I had nothing to lose. I got to the crib and crashed for an hour and some change.

Seven o'clock came around with the quickness. I showered up, threw on a polo and some jeans, and began the thirty minute trip up North. This time, it wasn't quiet at all. I had my zone out song of "Late Night Tip" by 3 6 knocking in the whip. Unlike many other nights, it wasn't all hot and muggy. There was a nice, cool breeze. It was still about 85, but it felt more of a cool summer night like I was back in the D. It took me back to the time my cousin Edward took me for the first real ride of my life. I was thirteen, almost fourteen. The year was 1998. I was starting my freshman year in high school in a few short weeks. Edward figured he was gonna break me into the grown people of the world.

"Cuz, tonight you start your growth process. I'm gone start showing you some real bitches." I was excited. I aint know where the hell we were going. Finally, we ended up at Belle Isle Beach. As a kid, this was your manhood check. We dreamed about the day we could be grown and roll through Belle Isle in our own whip, hollin' at the females and being involved with the mischief that it brought. We passed by hoards of women, car clubs, van clubs, more women, even more women, and an assortment of just niggas. It wasn't too many places where black folks could congregate at and not have anything pop off. However, with the amount of women that were out on the Isle, you really didn't have to worry about anything. That was my introduction to the preview of the real world. Now, I was living in it. Damn, I missed Eddie like a mutha.

I entered through the gates of Andersen and took that long death road down by the airfield. Busting that right and passing the church, I kept going until I hit the club they had. On first sight, I saw a gang of females outside in front of the joint. It was all chocolate and I damn sure didn't complain. I parked the whip, stepping out fresh, acting like I was a stranger who didn't know where he was at. All of 'em got quiet as I got to the door and entered my way in the joint. My shades were on, I was clean, and I know I had made an impression just by walking in. When I got to the main part of the joint, those shades disappeared quickly. This thing was packed with nothing but high quality lookin' women. I swear what they said was true. The Air Force definitely had nothing but pretty females in their ranks. I mean the ugliest chick I had noticed in here was a 9.5 on a 10 scale. Yes, it was that serious up in here.

"Good evening," as I turned around to see what I thought was a top ten sight.

"Huh?" I said, like I didn't hear her the first time.

"Hey, you performing tonight?" That's when I got in my smooth voice.

"Yea. Just put me on the list as Lamar." I extended my hand out to her.

"Cat," she said with a smile. "You looking pretty confident sir."

"Well that's how us boys from Detroit roll. We bred that way." Man I was on some cocky shit, and part of it was because of how fine she was.

"Aight. Well, since you so confident, how bout I put you up first?"

"I never go first, but in this case, I will," as I put the shades back on. It was obvious that we had hit it off, but I had to keep my pimp game to a minimum level. It was several bad breezies in here, so I didn't wanna jump off and snatch one too quick. I hit the bar and got me a pop. I may have been sippin' it like it was some Goose, but that's how good I felt right now. I made your favorite pop look beyond delicious. Remember what I just said as well. It's pop, not no damn soda. If anyone ask me to get them a soda from the store, I'm coming back with some Arm & Hammer.

"Alright y'all. Welcome to our first A.A.H.A. Conscious Open Mic Night. Look, we gone get right into it with a brother who, umm, I had the pleasure to meet face to face earlier." I heard the girls make their lil noises wondering who she was talking about. I just put my head down and smiled. I was that nigga right now.

"Ladies, I must admit, I ain't seen him round here, but he is fine. Y'all give it up for Lamar." I felt like these women were staring a hole through me as I walked up from the back. In my mind, I was walking on a red carpet, with flashing bulbs coming at me from all directions. I just hoped Kanye didn't come out and interrupt me saying that Beyonce had the best walk on the red carpet of all time. I got up on stage and grabbed the mic from Cat real slow, making sure that our eyes locked. She was giving me that you can get it all god damn night look. I damn sure wanted to give it to her.

"Aight. Ummm…how y'all doin'?" I needed to stop with this deep voice shit. The way these broads reacted in the crowd though, I was gonna try to mess around and get me a permanent Barry White.

"Well, like the very beautiful Cat said, I am Lamar." I made sure to make eye contact with her. Man I hoped she knew how beautiful she was. Sometimes you meet those girls who are fine to death, but think they are ugly because guys tend to not talk to 'em, not for their attitude, but just in general.

"I got this piece for y'all. I call it (as I looked at her), BLACK WOMAN."

BLACK WOMAN

"See, I like that they're what they call woman, that tanned
woman, that what you refer to as black woman,
that dark skin, lite skin, red bone, yella bone, mocha,
peanut butter, dark chocolate, so black that if she lay down
in the middle of the street, she look like a pothole type
woman, that show me what's up with life type woman, that
keep her hair done without a million colors type woman,
that pretty smile having ass woman, that child bearing hips
having ass woman, that pretty feet for sucking toes woman,
that cook me some shrimp and grits with a lil twist of cheese
type woman, that mix that Kool-Aid up with the right
amount of sugar type woman, that leave a nigga alone when
the game on type woman, that lock me down for the long
haul type woman, but the key to rollin with me is you gotta
be all woman…
See, if I want samples, I'll go to Albertson's on a Saturday.
I want us two way with that four play, add that up to make
love six days, and on the seventh we rest, and I hope you get
the math, and if you don't, I can break this down in simple
English….
She says get in between me like the word mine, and make
her mine and fuck her mind and make her mind explode like
a mine if I don't mind, and I'm losin' my mind cause her
body is mine, that pussy is mine, those titties are mine, and
my mind is going crazy from all these damn mines, but I will
continue the story if y'all don't mind. Now do y'all mind?

.....Thank you. See, I just love women period. Keyword: women. I don't deal with no rats all out for a brother's cheddar cause I'm better than that, and even though I'm black, I'm fluent in six different vernaculars. She think she slick when she talkin' that foreign language, that pig latin, but I don't fuck with swine, nor do I fuck with the other white meat. See, vanilla is rich, but I'm a chocolate fiend, and the only time this chocolate is dipped in vanilla is when a nigga goes to Dairy Queen, and if you still don't know what I mean, it's simple. I don't fuck with the snow, I left that shit back in Chicago, but I do mess with that black ice cause black is nice, black is tight, black is an ass that's phat and a pussy so ripe that it should be sold in cans for free, 99 per ounce. See, I like that type of black woman that sat in Egypt eating grapes, not these sisters more concerned with bathing apes, steady hollin' they want their George of the Jungle, but yet they stay on their monkey shit, jumpin' from dick to dick like the vine in the trees, and they dividing their trees letting penetration come at ease, so I'll keep my seeds cause ain't no point planting my roots in some tainted soil........
See, don't gimme spoils or leftovers. Give me a black woman who ain't gotta come over, she just cums over and over, in the same bed she resides with her man on a nightly basis. That's the one I call..wife."

"Thank you."

I got the loudest cheer I ever heard from any group of females in my life. The only time women screamed like this is if an ol' dusty faced llama breath ass nigga walked in trying to holla. I know I had their pussies wet. They were gonna mess around and have to call the fire department up in here for flooding. The one thing I learned about poetry is that when you spit a piece about love or women, especially black women, they all think that you're talking about them. I walked off that stage like my dick had grown four more inches on the spot. I responded to the ladies with thank you's as I made my way to the wall where Cat was. Luckily, there were multiple MC's for the event so we had a chance to chill.

"Did you like it?" She smiled.

"Nah. I loved it." Her girls beside her were hushed, but the looks on their faces said it all.

"You wanna go get something to eat after this is over?"

"Nope! She will leave right now. Bye Cat!" That was one of her homegirls pushing her up on me in a funny way. I thought it was hilarious, but she turned to me and said,

"Yea, let's roll." We walked up out of there and just began conversation. She was from Bradenton, Florida. I swear the chicks that I had met from that state were top notch. Did we go anywhere? Nah. We sat in the car just choppin' it up. This was rare. I was so used to leave, maybe get a bite to eat, and then you knock her cervix back. She was actually talking intellectually and stimulating my mind. Chalk it up to me getting older, or just me not conforming to the norm anymore.

"So, where's your man at?"

"In the passenger seat if he gives me good reason over time." It was a bold statement that she said and I liked it. A confident woman is a plus in my book.

"So who's to say I'm gonna be with you? What if I just want a friend to talk to?"

"Men don't talk the way you did about women who they just want as friends. You want what's under these clothes, and as a woman, I knew within the first five seconds of meeting you whether I would give you some or not. Now, that's for you to work for and not me. The ball's in your court. I'm 100% woman. I'm trying to see if you are 100% man." Baby girl was playing chess, not checkers. I liked her game. She was the bishop moving diagonally. I was the pawn. I was merely protecting the real me until I knew when to bring it out.

"I tell you what. How bout me and you link up next week for some dinner and dancing to see how 100 you are?" She smiled, showing all of those pearly whites.

"So you asking me out?"

"No, I'm telling you how you're gonna be occupied next weekend. 671-797-0353. Call me Saturday morning so you'll have something to think about over the next six days. Later beautiful." I exited the car like a boss and went to my own whip not looking back. I got to the whip and peeled out into the breezy Guam night. I don't know if I screwed up or just left her mind on cloud nine thousand. All I knew is that I was in feel good mode, and this brother's night was just starting. About 15 minutes later, I whipped it down to Zen Lounge. The blue lights gave it a mystic glow. Tonight, there was a good crowd up in that joint. I eased it over to the bar, settling for a simple cranberry juice, cause a brother didn't drink while he was driving. I came too far to even risk losing everything over a few drinks. The DJ was satisfying my ear canal as some old Erykah Badu and Common was making love to the speaker system. People were dancing, chillin on the couches, conversing, laughing, joking, and here I was, by myself, at one with myself.

Sometimes it takes separating from the rest of the world to find yourself in the world. With everything that transpired today and throughout the week, it was good to toast to myself. As humans, we complain about a lot of shit. I'm guilty of it just like the next man. When you realize that you are still breathing and have a chance to make your life better with every passing minute, then there is nothing you have to complain about. I chugged three more cranberry joints before I dipsetted out, headed to the crib to enjoy my bed.

Monday came around and my mood was back to being salty. I thought I would be down here to help people run their systems and train them up, however, that was all a bunch of bull. What they really wanted me to do was sit behind a desk and implement programs to train personnel. I wouldn't be working face to face. I would just be making necessary tools for future programmers and analysts to use. All I could hope was that someone would show them properly how to do things because learning through a computer wasn't always the solution for everything. Time passed slowly and the days dragged on. Thursday hit and it was the same ol', same ol'. This time though, I brought my notebook to work with me. As 10 a.m. hit, I was done with all my tasks for the day. I wasn't gonna clock out early because I wasn't gonna lose out on free money. I cracked my notebook open and just flipped through the pages. Everything was blank until I found what I wrote in it a while back. **'BANDAGES 2.'** One word and one number. I quickly scratched out the two and just concentrated on the title in front of me. *Bandages,* I thought. I couldn't comprehend a story to go along with it. I had writer's block like a mutha. Just then, my phone buzzed. It was Cat.

"You left my mind boggled. No man has ever did that to me. I look forward to Saturday." I didn't even respond to her. I was gone let a brother stay on her mind some more before I hit her up. I went back to what I was doing. I opened up a word document on my computer, eyes cutting back and forth from the screen and the notebook. BANDAGES...blank screen. BANDAGES...blank screen. BANDAGES...blank screen. I typed four words.

"Healing begins with writing."

From that moment on, I would write 1,663 words a day in memory of the first slave revolt that occurred in Gloucester County, VA. I figured if I was gonna write a book, then I might as well use a rarely talked about piece of history as my motivation. I let my fingers simply glide across the keyboard and begin my story.

"Blaze that shit up nigga!!" Yea, that was a helluva way to start off a story wouldn't you agree? I was pretty much done in about 20 minutes. I stared in amazement of what I had written so far. I know telling a story is a unique gift to have. Putting it into something that everyone can read and feel though, that was legendary. Writing taught me something valuable about life. As you write, you create. The more you write, the greater your creation becomes. The same goes for us in life. The more you live, the more great things you create. I had a feeling that this opportunity would truly show me a gift that I hadn't noticed my whole life. Yes, I wasn't used to not directly working with people. Sometimes, though, God shows us a fork in the road to take when we think we are headed in the right direction on the highways that we were accustomed to traveling.

8 VENUS VS. MARS

Cat: "So where are we meeting at?"

Me: "Lol. I thought I was gonna pick you up."

Cat: "Assuming certain moves is what caused Kings to lose empires. Ask the people of Troy."

Me: "Oh you a smart one huh?"

Cat: "No, I'm a challenging one."

I never thought a series of text messages could cause a battle of the minds, but this conversation did just that. Honestly, I can't front. I was kind of intimidated. I never faced a woman like this. It was a cat and mouse game where we weren't chasing each other. We were seeing who was gonna make the first move. We eventually agreed to meet up that night at Gecko's Nightclub inside The Reef Hotel on the Tumon Strip. The Masonic Brothers were throwing an all white party on GP. I had fucked with them for a good minute while being on this island. I have to admit, they were some real men. I didn't buy into all the devil worship talk or any other bullshit people said about them. What I seen were a group of men who were attempting to make the world a better place. I couldn't blame people for their assumptions, though. People always feared what they didn't understand. It was the human way. The jump off wasn't kicking off until nine o'clock and it was only one something. I pulled out my all white Dickies fit and threw some sharp creases in the top and bottoms. I pulled out the all white L.A. Dodgers fitted. When it came to the shoes, though, a brother was hurting.

"FUCK!!!," I yelled. My low cut Adidas were past their prime. It would've been easy to just give 'em a good deep cleansing, but who in the hell was I fooling? If I was gonna be fresh, it had to be from head to toe. It was time to get my shoe game right. I shot up north to Micronesia Mall to rock up in Foot Locker. I strolled in there, immediately catching the eyes of the local females. They were gazing at me, but they weren't anything that I was trying to look at.

"How are you today?"

"I'm good," I told the clerk. I had to admit, she actually looked decent for a local chick.

"So what you looking for today?"

"All white AF ones. Size 15." She took a step back, scanning me up and down.

"You joking right?"

"Baby, the only jokers I know are in a deck of cards. Now do you have what I need?" I swear my mouthpiece was slicker than corn oil on a flat top grill.

"Lemme go check," she said with the biggest smile on her face. As I waited, my phone buzzed.

"I see you. So what you getting me?" It was Cat. I started looking around like crazy. My eyes scanned the whole entire store, outside the store, nothin'. Where was this girl at? My joint buzzed again.

"Lol. This funny lookin' at you searching for me." I was starting to get mad in a crazy way. This girl was messing with my mental.

"Here are your shoes big man." I smiled at her.

"Indeed. I am a big…man." I walked away from her to sit down and try on my joints. I ain't even look back. I knew she was wet like my jumper on the basketball court.

"Hey!!" I turned around to see Cat.

"Girl, where the hell were you?"

"I was in the back at the House of Hoops section lookin' for some jump offs. So what you get me?"

"Dinner. At my place. Right after we leave here. That's what I got you. Whether you accept is depending on how many clothes I got left on inside of your head." She couldn't say shit as I kept my eyes locked on her for an additional five seconds and went back to my shoes.

"Well in my mind, what I see isn't impressive. Much better has infatuated my eyesight." She was truly a master of the comeback. I couldn't even knock it.

"Well I'm bout to pay for these. Where you gone be?"

"The Reef tonight at nine. See you there." She walked out and left me stunned. I was getting beat at my own game. I wasn't used to this, but it was showing me that I needed to sharpen things up. I paid for my joints and walked out the store confused. No woman had ever did this to me. Why was I taking this so serious? It was probably the fact that ever since I missed out on Kamilah, I didn't take any woman serious. As I waltzed through the parking lot, I damn near got hit by a car for walking so slow. The lady said something to me in whatever language she was speaking, but I truly wasn't giving a damn. My mind was heavy. This shit wasn't supposed to be happening to me. I did the chess playing and right now, this girl had made a move and put me in a position where I couldn't even get out of the position that I was trying to play. That bishop had turned into a queen and the pawn had turned into a rook. Checkmate.

The time was a little bit after five when I got home. I made a stop along the way to get a couple of C2's and some sunflower seeds. Walking back in my building, I decided to stroll down to the pool to see who was out and about.

"NIGGA!!!" I was shocked. The whole pool and barbecue area was packed.

"Man, when y'all niggas was gonna tell me y'all was having a barbecue?" The homey Lo smiled with that slick ass pimpin' mode behind it.

"Man bruh, we just kickin' it on the spontaneous tip. I wasn't even gone do this. I was bored, called the homey and threw some meat on the grill I had in the freezer for a while." Lo was my dude, a master G from North Carolina and a master of knowledge. He was like me. He equaled the amount of fun he had with double the amount of knowledge he learned. I could definitely dig that. A lot of the Navy cats I knew were out here, including a few dumb broads.

"Lo, where that boy Perk at?" He just started laughing as he pointed over towards the ocean to see him and a shorty coming up the steps.

"That boy banged her in the trees down there man. You know how these hoes from Cell Block 40 get down." He was right. Cell Block 40 was a code name for one of the Navy ships out here. That place indeed was full of girls who would get loose at the drop of a dime. I spent the next hour smashing on ribs and chicken while watching the rest of those boys get white boy wasted over the domino table. I went up to the house at about 6:30, plopping on the couch and cutting on the TV. I wanted some relax time before I did my dirt for the night. As I flipped through the channels, I came across a hood classic, JUICE. It was on the part where Q was holding Bishop up from falling off the roof. I was locked in. After he dropped, Q put the hoodie back on. Right then and there, my heart dropped. I had seen this joint a million times, but seeing a hoodie and relating that shit back to the cat riding his bike in the D before my cousin got murked gave me chills. I guess that's how it was, though. You see a black man in a hoodie and that's a sign that some bad shit is about to go down. I got caught up in my own zone for a minute. The eventful day, convos with Cat and everything else went to the wayside. I was in the dark mentally once again. This time, it was difficult to come out of. I reminisced on the last time I seen death first hand and it had me shook. My palms eventually met my face to collect my sorrows. Memories could break the strongest of men sometimes, and I indeed was being broke down. I silenced the TV and just collected myself for twenty minutes or so. As the sun began to set, I looked out the patio window and saw my life dwindle down with it. Just then, my phone buzzed.

"Fun. Tonight with me. Right when you leave the house. That's what you have tonight. Whether you accept is dependent on how much I am inside of your head." I could do nothing but laugh as she used my own words against me. It was like God seen me suffering and gave me healing through laughter. The hurt was still there, but life goes on. Tonight, it would go on in the form of fun. How much fun? That was yet to be determined.

Nine o'clock came and I made my last minute adjustments in the mirror. I was strict on myself when it came to my dress game. I took a fingernail clip and removed every loose fabric I found. The lint roller was in full effect as I had to make sure no dust was present. With a last spray down of my fitted, I was good to go. I strolled out the house feeling one hundred thousand. The Thallium cologne had me smellin' like a million bucks. Couldn't nann brother on this island touch me tonight. Just then, Cat texted me.

"I'm never impressed with a man who is late. Early is on time." This girl was really something else as I put my phone back in my pocket. I guess all colored people didn't operate on CPT. She was trippin', I thought. It wasn't like I was gonna get there and it was gonna be packed wall to wall. I took the back road by the hospital towards the strip. As I made that initial turn past Guam Memorial, or Get Ur Ass Murdered Hospital, seeing that they were highly in debt and your chances of survival were minimal, I slowed to see EMT's rushing in a patient, holding bags and all sorts of equipment over him. His people were behind him, crying and hysterical. It looked like he had been shot, which was rare out here. Hell, since I had been out here, there were only two murderous incidents. There was the local who threw his wife off a third floor balcony after he found out she was cheating on him with a Navy cat. Then there was the crazy nut who drove into a crowd of Japanese tourists, got out the car, and stabbed them. In that incident, 13 people ended up losing their lives. That was it. For the most part, it was chill out here.

I got back rolling to normal speed, which was 35 out here. I hit the roundabout to the strip and soaked in everything. I passed G Spot, one of the strip clubs out here, California Pizza Kitchen, which was my spot of spots, and Churrascos, the Brazilian Steak House, which I had conquered many of nights. Shit was gravy from what I seen. The strip was packed beyond belief tonight. *Oh yea,* I thought. Tonight was gonna be epic. Finally, I got to the The Reef and parked. The first sight I seen...a gang of chocolate bunnies exiting the car in all white. I almost forgot how fine Cat was looking at all these stallions.

"Excuse me?," the sweetest voice said as I shut my car door and turned around. "You did that poem at the base last week right?" All her homegirls were now behind her, undressing me with their eyes. I was nervous as hell.

"Yea, that's me." If this were a group of niggas, I'd be swingin. Four bad ones surrounding you though, and all of them wanting you, that's a whole different ball game. She looked me up and down, biting her lip.

"Well, talk to me later. I might want that poem spit to me in a private setting." They all gave me the eye as they walked away, headed inside the hotel. I could tell this night was gonna be more than epic. I took a deep breath and walked up towards the hotel entrance. Somebody or some people were doing it big as a stretch Cadillac Limo was parked right out in front. I walked in, amazed at the interior of this place. Much like other hotels on the strip, this was for those folks who wanted the upscale experience. I looked around the whole initial floor and couldn't find anything.

"Excuse me miss?," I asked the desk clerk. "I'm looking for the all white party inside Geckos."

"Down the wide stairs sir, make a right by the pool and it's inside of Geckos Nightclub." I felt like a num nut. When I walked back over, there was a big ass sign saying Geckos Nightclub downstairs. I walked down, out and past the lit up heated pool. Immediately, I heard the music blaring. Waka Flocka "No Hands" was getting my mood started. As I stepped foot inside, I seen that everyone else's party had begun by the time that I left the house. This place was packed to the max. Everyone was clean as well. Shit, I felt out of place like all to be damned. Here I am in an all white Dickies joint with AF ones and all these gentlemen and ladies in here were dressed to the T; vests, suits, slacks, Kangols, fedoras. This was grown folks shit to the max.

"Glad you could make it bruh." I turned around to see Puncho.

"What's poppin' my guy?," as we dapped up like G's.

"A, I don't even have to explain earlier. You know I don't challenge those who have nothing to offer. That should tell you something bruh. The objective is to become pure of mind in the midst of chaos. What was going through your mind today was chaos when I was talking to you. I ain't by no means perfect, but I do try to play my part in keeping my brothers together. Remember, once you understand the universe, it gives you the key to life. Once you have the key to life, your work has just begun. Now go and have some fun man. Matter fact, first drink is on me." I dug everything bruh had just spit to me. The funny thing is that we were around the same age, but he had the mindset of the damn Buddha I swear. He always talked about traveling the world to find the Zen Master, trying to find what was truly in his spirit. I could definitely respect that.

"Hennessy and Coke, beautiful," I told the bartender. As me and Puncho sat back waiting for our drinks, I felt two hands come around my stomach.

"Welcome," as I turned around to see Cat. We embraced in a hug which felt more than just friendship.

"Here bruh." Puncho handed me my drink. "Handle your business. Miss lady, I assure that you have made a wise choice." She laughed as bruh nodded his head and headed off into the party to do his own thing.

"You're late," she said.

"Well," as I took the first sip of my medicine. "That depends on what your definition of late is. Am I late for this party or late coming into your life? The way I see it, to be late is to not start in a designated time. Our time started last week, designated by something higher than both of us. So how am I late if you did not realize that?" She backed up, looking at me like who in the hell was this dude. I just played it cool and sipped my Henn Dog, waiting for her response. I probably had her pussy wetter than Niagara Falls.

"Well in this instance, Mr. Atteley, I'm wrong. You got me." I just smiled as we chopped it up by the marble clad bar that stretched around on all sides. We kicked it for a good minute, choppin' it up, until "that song" came on. "C'mon Detroit. Let's see how y'all do it." She grabbed my hand.

I had never heard anything about a 'Drunk In Love,' but it quickly became an all time favorite of mine. Some classic Silkk had been blazed by the DJ right after that. Damn, this felt good. In the Midwest, we rocked to R&B at a lot of our functions. Twerking was cool, but sometimes you just wanted to get close to a woman and feel her embrace. We made it to the middle of the dance floor. Everybody was out here groovin'. Cat slowly placed my hands around her waist as she began to move her body against mine. The vibe was right. She could definitely move that thang. For the slender type body that she had, her booty was in another league of its own. We took our dancing through Silkk, Dru Hill, Az Yet and all of the classic groups of the 90's. It reminded me of basement parties at the crib. You find that one girl who could throw it good and you just locked her down. There was no conversation. We let our bodies do the talking. Hers were telling me she enjoyed this. Mines was saying I wanted to do more than dance. Naw, this wasn't like The Wood. I ain't get hard like Mike. I did, however, get aroused like him in the sense that the woman I was with was probably one of the most beautiful creations of God that I had ever seen. After the end of 5 songs, she turned around to me, face to face.

"You move pretty well Mr. Atteley." I chuckled at that notion.

"It's not that I move well. It's just that I know what I'm doing."

"Do you really?" I looked up towards the ceiling as if to say I'm bout to get her God.

"Yea," in the deepest, smoothest voice I ever spoke in. She just smiled, showing off those perfect pearly whites. Y'all just don't know how good it is to rock with a woman who had some good dental benefits. We walked off the dance floor, loungin at one of the side booths for the rest of our time. By the time I had looked at my watch it was 12:22.

"So, how is this for a date night?" Those cat like eyes looked at me like she was plotting to kill me when I least expected it. She grabbed my face in between those soft hands of hers slowly, but passionately, placing a soft kiss to my lips. My mind was going into overdrive now. This girl's mouth was like touching soft bread fresh out of the oven.

"That's my answer." It was a helluva answer and one I could dig.

"So where do we move from here?," I asked her. Her eyes stayed locked with mine. There was a story she was about to tell me.

"We stop. There is no more."

"Whatchu mean?," as I softly placed my middle and index finger to her chin.

"I deploy in two weeks, and I can't commit to you like I should. I would be wrong to have you wait for me." My eyes stayed locked with hers. I soaked in everything she told me. If this was ten years ago, the young acting Lamar would've said "fuck this" and found him another broad. This grown man, though, responded like a grown man should.

"Let me apologize to you. I'm only here for two years. I have the option to extend permanently if I want to, but I don't think I will do that. You are a prize catch. Our lives are on two different paths and I respect yours. Don't look at this as bad news. Look at it as you have found someone to confide in for a long time." No words were said as we just looked at each other. We were in a hypnotized trance of some sorts. Damn, this was like Kamilah all over again. I didn't even get buck to "Grove St. Party" which was playing, and Lord knows that was my song that I had to be on the dance floor for.

"You ready to leave?," she asked me.

"Not without you."

"Who said you were leaving without me?"

"Who said I was leaving with you?," I responded. This chess game was fun. We both knew our intentions, but we constantly tried to challenge each other. We stopped by the photo booth on the way out to snap a few crazy photos. Making our way up the stairs and to the lobby, I saw Puncho and my dawg Pine, who we all called "Chicago." Puncho raised a glass of champagne at me as I nodded my head back at him. Me and Cat were out the door headed to our whips.

"You wanna get a bite before we head in beautiful lady?" She looked at me as she hit the remote on her key to unlock her car.

"We'll eat breakfast in the morning after we wake up. Follow me." She gave me that look as she got in her car. I jumped in mine, started it up and followed her out the lot. The night temperature was perfect and all was well. After a good fifteen minute drive, we pulled up to her condo complex. She came back to meet me at my car, seeing that I was in the visitor's parking lot which was a good ways from the door.

"You don't sleep wild do you?," she asked.

"Only when I haven't been active. After a good workout, I'm out like a baby."

"Oh yea," she said. "You will definitely sleep like a baby tonight," as we walked towards the doors.

"Look up Lamar. See? That bright star is Venus. It's the brightest in the night sky."

"That's where y'all women are from right?"

"Most women. I'm from parts unknown."

"Well maybe I will figure out those parts," as we walked into the elevator. She just looked at me, cracking a smile and gigglin'. As the doors opened to her floor, she answered my question.

"Yea. You will." We walked to the middle of the hall, arriving at her joint. She opened the door and walked in.

"Lock the door behind you. Both locks." I took a glimpse down both ends of the hall before I shut the door. Why did I grin at the door across from hers like it was a mirror? I really didn't know. What I did know is that I was about to sleep like a baby. I closed her front door. Goodnight world.

9 SUMMER OF SIN

Months had flown by. I had finished my book that I was writing entitled **BANDAGES** while sitting in that office for months on end. In that time from January to July, I had gotten so much done that it seemed like I was literally on a seven month vacation. I mean hell, making training programs and sending them off to other people was as easy as pulling a hooker in Las Vegas. Vegas...Vegas.....hot damn Las Vegas. I had about nine months left on this island before I was due to be back.

That option to extend wouldn't even be an option for me, as no amount of money could keep me on this island. It was time to head back to my adopted hometown for a good month. This vacation was much needed. It was the beginning of August and I couldn't picture any better way to ring in my 29th birthday than with bright lights, bad women, bomb booze, and the occasional street show put on by the local crazies. Yea, this would definitely get my juices flowing. One month of freedom and just no fucks given. Hell, I even had plans to shoot on down to Palm Springs and Newport Beach in Cali for a few days to unwind down there.

August 1st had finally crept on up. It was a chill Thursday and this airport was emptier than a Montreal Expos game back in the day. That was cool with me as I could bounce on through security and get on this quick hop to Tokyo. Seeing that this would be my first adventure back to the states, I had to do it big on those boys. The airport here was laced with high end stores so it was only right that I got some high end gear for myself. Burberry watch, check. $400 Burberry polo, check. Prada shades, check. A nigga was gravy now. I didn't need to buy up the entire country. Hell, it wasn't even my style to buy anything that expensive unless it was a suit. However, sometimes, you had to live a little bit.

My money was straight so I had no worries at all. I boarded my damn near empty flight and just kicked back. It would be a short four hours so a good nap would be in effect. I was leaving on a Thursday and arriving in America on a Thursday so I would need all the sleep I could get. We took off and I knocked out. It seemed like as soon as I closed my eyes, we were landing. Narita Airport was big as all to be damned. It could've been it's own mini city to be real with you. I pulled out $40 dollars and exchanged it at the money exchanger: 3,000 Yen. I took me a few pics for the 'book, knowing damn well half the folks wasn't gonna know what I was holding in my hand. They would really think I was living like a king. Shit!!! This was food money and nothing more.

I stopped across from my gate to indulge in some of those fire ass noodles. I couldn't pronounce the name of the dish, but all I knew was that it had shrimp in it. Me and shrimp went together like stocking caps and waves. Screw those chopsticks, too. I was American. All I knew was a fork. It did the job, too, as I smashed this entire bowl. I never thought an airport could give you an out of body experience. I was in a different world, but I really felt like I was out of this world. Planes didn't use to be my forte, and that was all due to how many of those joints went down on a regular basis. You go back to TWA Flight 800 which was shot down and I don't care what anyone says. You got planes that just fly up and disappear, which ironically have a bunch of top notch world scientists and other high figures aboard. The shit was so easy to see and I didn't wanna be the next victim because someone wanted to fulfill an agenda. However, one good thing that came out of that is that I had no fear of actually living. All I could do was try and do right everyday. When it's all said and done, I would hope my maker says "Good Job," and let me through the gates. After an hour of waiting, it was time to board and make the 11 hour and some change flight. I had done it before so it was nothing to do it again. The only thing that made it better this time around was the fact that I was returning to the states. The kid was back on his way to his home soil and he was gonna tear some shit up while he was there.

Eleven hours passed and we had about 20 minutes until we landed in L.A. Crazy as it may sound, I had already adjusted back to the time difference. I left Guam at eight in the morning on August 1st and I was back in the states at 7 a.m. August 1st. We landed smoothly into LAX, then proceeded with the 15 minute terminal ride on the plane to our gate. The fact that I could cut my phone on and get service like normal was gravy. I didn't need any bum ass Guam phone company. My Sprint joint was back to being my baby. After a God awful wait due to all these people, I rolled up off the plane and headed to the rental car station. I had forgotten how good American sisters looked. My head was turning like a corkscrew, loving everything I saw, except for the few round pounders that interrupted my vision. I didn't do big girls at all. I made it to Hertz, waiting patiently to get a whip. It would've been easy to just hop another flight to Vegas. It would've been a quick 45 minute trip, however, I wanted to drive on American roads, in an American Car, with an American middle finger waving at me for cutting someone off in traffic. It would be a four hour and some change ride, but it would definitely be worth it. First, though, I had to make a stop.

L.A. wasn't my stomping grounds, but I knew some good people down here and it behooved of me to visit them while I had the chance to. I shot out towards the freeway, heading right over towards 21st and Labrea. A community figure named Andre was well respected out here. He had done a lot for the L.A. community and I had met him some time back through his daughter, who I swear I would wife up if I had the chance. She was a DJ and she was beautiful. I jumped off on Manchester, coming off the freeway, and made my way to his house. The drive made me think about a lot, particularly the crib.

L.A. was just like Detroit. It was plagued with drugs, crime, gangs and death. The only thing that was different was how they operated out here. That was every hood, though.

We can front like our hood was harder than the next. In truth, we all faced the same plagues. The only thing that differed between all of us was the lingo and the dress code. I pulled up to his house, which stood out from the rest, with the huge black F150 sitting on those thangs in front of it. To the side was a black and chrome Harley. I had never been a fan of riding motorcycles, but I had to admit, some of those joints made me want to jump on one and ride all throughout the country. I parked on his narrow street and walked up to the door. I rattled three knocks upon the screen doors which seemed to litter every house in L.A.

"Well hello, sir."

"Hello miss lady." It was his daughter Marie. She was 5'4 with a pretty face and a bangin' body to match. I walked on in, eyes locked on that plump booty of hers. Man, she just didn't know. If she was my wife, man I would be devouring that on a nightly basis.

"Daddddddddddddddddd," she called out. I patiently waited in the living room, looking at the opaque pictures on the wall. "He's coming," she told me, peeking her head around the wall, giving me that pretty smile of hers. I think she liked me. Hell, I hoped she liked me.

"Young man. Young man." That was Andre coming around the corner. "How's everything sir?" We embraced in a hug. It was really good to see him. "Come over here to the dining room table. Let's chat." We kicked back, 'Dre pouring up some wine he had on stash. "You know, my daughter is available if you want her." All I could do was chuckle as she yelled

"Stop trying to hook me up dad," from the back room. He laughed hysterically. That was his nature. He was fun loving, yet down to earth. He loved his community and his people.

"So off my daughter and on to you. How's the overseas life treating you?" I gave him a novel of everything as he just sat there and listened to my tales of mischief. He sipped his wine very slow, taking in every word carefully. One thing about 'Dre, he took what you said exactly the way you said it. If you said a tree vine crip walked up Rodeo Drive with a dead serious tone, he would take it as you actually saw it. It wasn't that he was stupid, but he truly believed that all a man had was his word. If he was a real man, his words would not be full of lies and deceit. Time went on as we chatted back and forth, discussing life. Then, everything came to a stand still.

"Young brother. I'm in the early stages of cancer." My mouth dropped, my heart sank and my soul became crushed beyond belief.

"What you mean Dre?"

"Exactly what I said. I'm in the early stages of cancer." He was saying this like it was nothing, which was kind of bothering me.

"Why are you speaking about this like it doesn't matter? I don't get it." He laughed at me. It was a slap in the face kind of. That's when he hit me with the real.

"Look here. You know I'm a principal. I deal with young kids on a daily. I tell them every morning when I see them, that it's time to go to work. Well, just like I tell those kids to go to work, it's time for me to go to work and fight this. When sickness or any obstacle comes up in your life, you can either fight it, or let it kick your ass. I will fight this. Even if it kills me, I will fight it. Until I have no breath left in my body though, then I'm gonna live. You got that?"

I couldn't say a word. All I could do was nod my head in agreeance. When an OG, a true OG gives you words of wisdom, you soak it in. That's why I rocked with the old heads anywhere I was, whether Vegas, L.A. or anywhere. I could learn from them.

"Now, take my daughter out for me. She go with some young guy named Joe. I mean, he cool, but I think you'll be better." He must've knew she was coming down the hall to say that, cause I could see the joking manner written all over him. "Dad, Imma beat you up," as she put him in a playful headlock. I dug this man. Just seeing a father and daughter interact like they did was a blessing. You could tell he had been there her whole life. That's what many young girls, especially black girls, were missing in my generation. That father figure they needed was nowhere in sight. That's why so many of em grow up to be wildin' out and doing crazy shit that they know they have no business doing. If only all men would step up to the plate when creating a child, then this world would indeed be a better place.

I kicked it for about an additional 30 minutes before I said my goodbyes and got on the road to Vegas. It was a four hour ride that I would happily enjoy. It would give me time to just sit back and reflect on things in my life. My auntie knew that I was coming and I could guarantee some bomb food would be waiting for me. I got about an hour into my trip. I had cut the music off and just zoned out on the road. I didn't realize how much I really missed everything. More in particular, my family back East. My moms, pops, cousins, all them. It was the simple good times that I missed. Hell, the times we were on the road together were classic in my life. I really pondered on my mama more than anything. I really hated that she was miserable, however, she was too comfortable to leave an unhealthy situation. I used to drive myself crazy with this thought. That's until I realized that my mom had to find her own inner peace. Dad was just unemotional and I had really just given up on him. What I mean by that is I had given up on him ever telling me I love you. I had given up on him not being materialistic and feeling like he had to out do everyone. I gave up on him ever feeling like he was always right.

I loved him, I truly did, however, I knew that our relationship could be way better than it was. As a kid, it would have been cool to just do a lot of the simple stuff together that fathers and sons did. Some of those things we did and I was grateful. A lot of other things, they didn't happen. It pained me inside and I would probably never be over it. For my own inner peace though, I quit letting it be a burden in my life a long time ago. In life, you are damned if you do and damned if you don't. I'll be damned if I let any of my past impair my future.

I got to the outside of the strip at exactly 3:38. I swear on everything I love, seeing the Stratosphere was the greatest shit ever. I let out a big ass yell as I was finally home.

"WADDUP LADIES!!!," I yelled at a group of white girls in a Lexus on the freeway. They looked at me like I was the craziest mofo in the world. I didn't care, though. Vegas had missed me and I had missed it. It was time to get it in on level ten thousand. Finally, after what seemed like forever, I pulled up to my aunt's house. There was my Uncle Berry outside, taking the trash out.

"Nephew!!!," he yelled out, throwin' his hands up in the air. I got out the car full of excitement. Puddles ran her lil ass over there, circling around me like I was a damn fire hydrant.

"Sup unc???," as we embraced in a hug.

"Man let's get in this house. It's hotter than scorpion nuts out here and ya auntie been waiting for you." We stepped into a giant ice box as the A/C was on polar bear frost.

"Hey nephew," as she continued to play games on her computer.

"You aint gone get up and hug me auntie???"

"Nigga if you don't walk yo young ass over here. I'm the elder."

"Well I'm the sexy one in the family." She just stared at me.

"Nigga please." We both laughed as I walked over and gave her a hug for the ages. It felt good to see them both. I survived long enough to have this moment again. I raided the fridge for some orange juice and leftover chicken wings. I heated 'em up and sat down back in the living room where they were. I went on for at least a good hour, telling them the stories of what Guam had given me, how it had changed me, and how it had made me better. Most of all, how it had made me appreciate the things that we had here in America: Walmart, Target, Sally's Beauty Supply. Every city got a Sally's, and y'all can kiss my ass if you say I'm lying. 6:00 came with the quickness. I hadn't even realized we were talking so long.

"So what you doing tonight?," my aunt asked.

"I'm down for the count auntie. I done been halfway round the globe, to LA, and now here, all in a span of almost 36 hours. I am beat the hell up and I just wanna sleep like a rock tonight. I got 29 more days to create all the mischief I can."

"Well, you know where everything at. Me and Barry gotta work tomorrow so we'll be in bed in a couple of hours." From the looks of it, it looked like my uncle was well on his way as he was laid back in his recliner watching TV. He was known for falling asleep in that thing and tonight probably wasn't gonna be any different.

"Did you bring me any sideways back nephew?"

"Yo dick gone be on the side of the road hangin from the side of a tree nigga." There they went, my aunt and uncle. I knew it was just jokes, but it never ceased to amaze me how kid actin' they were.

"I'll be back y'all. I'm gonna get these bags out the car and chill for the night." I walked out the house and let out a great sigh. I took in the air from the Nevada mountains and was so appreciative for being back here. Everything was so peaceful. A nice summer breeze had crept through, which was rare for this time of year. Summers in Vegas were scorchers. As I grabbed my bags from the trunk, my phone rang. At first I was shocked like who in the hell was calling me from Guam. Then I remembered I had my Sprint phone back on.

"Hello?"

"BOY, WHY YOU AIN'T CALL ME WHEN YOU GOT IN?" It was my mama and she was hot. She had a right to be though. I sure as hell didn't call.

"Ma...Ma...I mean...Ma." That's all I managed to get out as she gave me an old fashioned ass chewing. She finally calmed down after about ten minutes of ranting and we actually had a good conversation. With that handled, I waltzed back into the house and began to unwind back in my room. A hot shower got me right. It felt good to just say that I was showering back in America. The water hit me different. It was like the dirt and grime of the last year and some change was slithering off of me and heading down the drain. I threw on some b-ball shorts and walked out to the kitchen to get me some more grub. The house was quiet, lights were out and they had retired to their bedroom. I know they say old folks go to sleep with the chickens, but they were right. It was only seven something and they were already in the bed. I kept it simple and just made me two grilled cheese sandwiches on the George Foreman grill. The simple things in life were what kept me going and this was no different. I took my plate back to the room, plopped on the bed, and cut on the TV to the news.

"There's a report coming in from North Las Vegas of a shooting at a residence. A seven year old girl was killed when two men began arguing on a porch. One man pulled out a gun and as the other man ran, he began shooting. He struck the man once in the leg, but at the same time, delivered a fatal bullet wound to the young girl who was riding her bike."

My heart instantly dropped as I couldn't even fathom what this young girl's family was going through at this time. Kids were nothing but mere innocence, and they deserved every chance to grow up and become something special. This made me think about one special little girl back home whose life was cut down in one of the most heinous acts ever committed by a group of men. Kamiya Gross was just two years old when men who I shouldn't even called men gunned her down. And for what? To send her father a message. You

kill a fucking two year old to prove that you are a gangster???
That aint being a gangster. That is being a **BITCH!!!**

In America, so many people forget about the cases like
this that happen way too often. We often get too wrapped up
in adult news. Whose album is blowing off the charts. Who
is sleeping with who. We focus so much on adult stories, yet
we forget about these kids, and I for one am sick of the shit.
I just cut the TV off and sat in the dark for a minute, fan
blowin' on me as I pondered my thoughts. What happened
didn't affect me personally as a part of their family. It did,
however, personally affect me as a human being. I was
transfixed, stuck in a literal state of shock. Right then and
there, I prayed to God.

"Lord,
I come to you as a giver,
much like You were when You gave your only Son.
I ask that you take a blessing from me
to give to this young girl's family.
May you take strength from me
to strengthen their family.
May your will be done
and comfort those who may not understand.
Allow my heartbeat to be theirs
and thank you for opening my vision
to something bigger than me.
In your Son Jesus name I pray……..
AMEN"

I felt obligated to say those words. This wasn't about me.
This was about me being there for my fellow human being.

More so, the victim was black. Not that it mattered what color someone was when they died, but with our mortality rate, I took it to heart. I just left the TV off and stared at the ceiling, hoping that God would just come through the roof and take me. Not in the literal sense, but take any remnants of the man I once was and throw him in the trash forever. I had grown up, and grown up is what I wanted to stay. I was far from perfect, and I would never be that way. However, striving for perfection is what was gonna keep me alive and I knew it. I closed my eyes and put night one in the books. My God, this fan felt good.

Saturday was now here and it was time to get it in. I was fully rested and rejuvenated. The time crunch was officially shaken off, even though it really didn't affect me to begin with. After having breakfast at the casino with the fam, I decided to spend the afternoon to myself, getting reacquainted with my city. As always out here, things were changing. New casinos were going up left and right. More housing developments were being established, seeing that this was the new land of opportunity. Vegas was that city to be quite honest with you. One o'clock was here, and the hunger games started to play in my stomach. I swung down to the end of the strip to bask in the glory of the Stratosphere buffet. This shit was always on point. Combine that with the fact that I could always catch a glimpse of people who had just came down from the top riding the big shot by the shocked looks on their faces. I dropped the twenty five plus dollar price and loaded up. Shrimp, crab legs, mussels, clams, salmon, more shrimp and steak. Yea I know, the kid was a seafood junkie. Things were well as I dug in, savoring the taste of the Pacific Ocean's finest cuisine. Just then, my phone rang. I looked at it and didn't recognize the number. In typical black folks fashion, I let it ring. We don't answer numbers we don't recognize. I kept eating and it rang again. I was wondering who in the hell was dialing my joint. I didn't know anyone from the 209 area code. I wiped my hands off real quick and googled that area code on my phone. Modesto and Stockton were just a few of the cities that popped up. Fuck it, I thought. I hoped whoever they meant to call wasn't gonna miss anything important.

Ringgggggggggg. Again, there it was. I was pissed now. I just went on ahead and picked it up.

Me: "Hello."

Person: "Lamar. It's your brother."

Me: "Jay Hall, Gump? Man quit playing. Who is this?

Person: "Like I said, it's your brother."

Me: "My nigga, I don't know who you looking for but......

Person: "The old heads call your pops LJ on the block."

Everything in the world stopped. The lump in my throat was the size of a human brain. My fork dropped to the plate in shock.

"My dude, how do you know this?"

"If you available, meet me at Hidden Falls Park in Henderson at six." He hung up. I didn't know what to think. Not anyone outside of the Eastside of Detroit and my family knew my pops' nickname. This shit was fucking with me something serious. I remember pops had told me a few times that I had a brother in California somewhere, but I put no emphasis on it. Hell, I had found out I had another sister when I was 16, but I didn't concern myself with her either. Now I was at a crossroads. I didn't know if this was legit or someone trying to set me up for the okedoke. I mean, this was Vegas, a mob ran town. People had ways of gettin back at you.

I didn't recall hurting or screwing over anyone in the past, but you never knew here. I left my food on the table and headed back to the parking lot. Once there, I sat in my car, A/C on blast, thinkin about what I had just heard. I sat there for a good ten minutes, just pondering on what I was gonna do. Then, I made up my mind. I was gonna take that risk. No gun, no knife, no associates, just me. I had to do this, even if it meant the worst possible outcome. I didn't wanna think like that, but I had to keep that thought in the back of my mind. From about 2:30-4:30, I lounged around on Fremont Street. I walked up and down taking in the happiness of the tourists and the crazy shows people put on down here. It actually put my mind at ease quite a bit, as one of the biggest moments of my life was upon me. 4:45 hit and I waltzed it back to my car. As I pulled up to the parking booth to pay, the woman said,

"God is about to reveal something to you," as she handed me my change.

"What makes you say that ma'am?" She smiled at me.

"I see an aura and a glow covering you right now. Something amazing is about to happen. God Bless." I smiled, nodded my head and peeled off. Those were great words to hear as I headed off to Henderson to meet up with this man who was claiming to be my family. My music of choice on this ride was some old Ghetto Mafia. 'I Can Feel It' was a zone out song for me when I was going through things and contemplating decisions. This right here was one of those times. I was excited, but nervous. I didn't know what to expect. As I pulled my car up to the park a full 30 minutes early, my heart rate increased dramatically. You would've thought I was getting married and not meeting my kinfolk. I calmed myself down, parked myself on a park bench and just waited patiently. No one else was here and it was sort of an eerie feeling.

My cap was to the back, chain around my neck, blue and white ones laced right. I felt like I was back in the hood, except it was actually beautiful. My mind drifted to my childhood for a minute. So many people on the block were my play brothers and sisters. We had each others back through thick and thin, 'cause that's what we had to do in order to survive the D. It was about ten of us total. Names weren't important, just the lives. From elementary all the way through high school, it was give and take with everything when it came to us. Now, looking back at everything and seeing that I'm the only one who is alive today, I just began to be grateful for everything and every lesson that allowed me to survive to the point where I was at today. My phone buzzed.

"Is that you on the park bench?" I looked up towards the parking lot. There was only one other car in the parking lot.

A royal blue BMW that was cleaner than a muthafucka. I just threw my arm up in the air, waving, letting him know that it was me. He got out the car. He was ways away, but I could tell he was a tall brother. He was at least 6'6. The closer he got, the more shit started to play inside of my head on how things were going to go. Finally, he got within 5 feet of me and just stopped.

"Lil bruh." I got up slowly, taking two steps forward. I was seriously looking at my twin. You could definitely tell that we had the same pops. All of our dad's features were all over us.

"Big bruh," as I continued to stare back at him. For about a minute, neither one of us took our eyes off each other. You would think we were sizing each other up for the fight of the century, like it was Mayweather vs. Pacquiao or some shit. However, I knew what this was. It was like looking at your mirror image.

"You mind if we sit and rap lil bruh?"

"Let's go," I responded. We sat on that park bench and the reunion was finally here. He pulled out an envelope and handed it to me.

"Open this." I looked at him as I opened up the manilla folder. I chuckled.

"Long Beach State huh?" Big bruh just smiled.

"Yea. I hooped for them four years straight. It was some of the best times of my life. I enjoyed that shit to the fullest." He paused for a minute. "You know I thought that was the most thrilling time of my life. Standing here now though, I see things different. I'm really here talking to you." We just locked eyes for what seemed like eternity.

"So why did pops leave you?" With a deep breath, I could tell I might just hear something that I didn't wanna hear.

"I never knew pops. I only knew what my moms told me. He was out there in LBC for a minute. For a good minute actually. They hit it off, she got pregnant and......I don't know what happened between the nine months I was being made in my mom's stomach, but they just fell off. I talked to him a few times, but it didn't last long at all. I didn't know much until I actually started searching out for you." He looked up towards the sky. I didn't even know what to say.

"Big bruh…how'd you find me?"

"I come out here for business about every three months for quarterly meetings. I go to LVAC, the athletic club out here. I was rappin with one of the trainers and he said I looked like one of his homeys. I asked him who and he said your name. I immediately thought about pops, asked him for your number and I took a chance. The way you reacted, I knew it was you. I don't know if you were searching for me, but the minute that I had a chance, I had to search you out to find some inner peace. This shit means the world to me right now lil bruh. Matter fact, lemme stop callin' you lil bruh. You Lamar. I'm Ty. I ain't big bruh. I'm just your brother." I tried to hold it in, but the tears started to flow down my face. I thought he was gonna crack some foul joke about me crying, but a simple hand placement on my left shoulder said more than any words that could come out of a humans mouth.

"It's aight Lamar. That shows you a man. Shit, how you think I felt? Nights I would lock myself in the bathroom crying, wishing that I even had a pops. Shit being in Long

Beach without a daddy, that shit can change a man something serious."

"Is that why you got that bright blue BMW?" He started laughing.

"Yea man, that's part of the reason. I got down with the Rollin 40's in LBC. Shit, my momma tried her damnedest, and she went to war to keep clothes on my back and food on the table. When those streets call though, you pick up. I did that shit up until I was about 23, til the fateful night that changed my life. There I was, sitting in the car blowing kush with some of my Crip niggas. I was a year removed from college. I had a degree, but I was still young and dumb, so I didn't wanna do shit with my life. Any who, we sitting on the corner of Walnut one night blazing big. We were all high as a kite, talkin' bout bitches and all sorts of other shit. I was in the back seat, my nigga Mo was shotgun, my nigga Will was in the driver seat and Brian was right next to me. In the midst of all the fun as we saw it, I looked out the window. A nigga with a black hoodie rode past the whip slow, locking eyes with me. Them other niggas in the car was so high in the sky they didn't even notice it. I followed him with my eyes as far as I could, 'til he was out of my vision totally. Right then and there my mind was telling me something bad was 'bout to happen. 'A Deuce Loc, hit this shit?' That was Will handing me the blunt back. Just as I grabbed it, I looked up and I swear I saw the grim reapers face in a hoodie right outside the window. Time slowed down dramatically as I seen that gun whip out. None of us had time to whip out the flame throwers. I seen the first spark and I knew it was over. Glass shattered everywhere. Blood curling screams were let out by everyone.

When the dust settled, I sat there clutching myself, beggin' God not to let me die. I didn't know it at the time, but I had been shot six times. Will and Mo were done. I leaned over, burning inside, to see Brian taking his last breaths, eyes glossy, lookin' in the sky. 'Brian,' I called out, while I was gasping for my own air. 'T-T-T-T-Take care of my son for me.' Those were his last words as he faded off, dying right there in front of me. I managed to open the door and slump out. Crawling on the concrete, I was hoping, praying that anyone had called the police, and that someone would help me. As I struggled to move, I saw a wheel stop right in front of me. I grabbed hold of it, lookin' up at a man in a black hoodie.

As I stared into his dark mystique, I knew it was all over for me. I continued looking, but I could see nothing. At least if I was gonna die, I wanted to look my killer in his eyes. Slowly, he pulled his hoodie off. I saw me. I saw me. Me and only me. Same blue rag and all. All I could do was look down and place my face to the ground. What I fought for the longest was gonna be the same thing that took me out. **HEYYY!!!!** Someone yelled that. I don't know who it was, but it saved my life. Dude on the bike took off and I never saw him again. When I came to the next time, I was in a hospital room, recovering slowly." Things got quiet between both of us. My bro had really been about that life. I was just glad to see he was gravy now. Most of all, I was happy that me and him were now on one accord.

"Well bruh, that's some shit. I aint never been thru that, but it's a lot that you need to know about me to fully understand me." He looked at me, giving me that chuckle.

"I got all the time in the world lil bruh. Let's hit my hotel lobby, kick back, have some drinks and catch up on what we missed out on all these years.....family." That last words spoke volumes in my blood. They say all blood ain't family and all family ain't blood. In this case, we were. Made by the same man, in different times, united through random circumstances. I can't even call it random though. I just call it divine intervention, because God indeed has a plan for everything. He planned me coming home this time to finally see the mirror image of myself. This was indeed a blessing. We didn't even make it back to the hotel on the strip. We stopped at a nearby sports bar, ate piles upon piles of wings and just caught up on everything. This right here made my vacation on point, and it was just the third day.

Day ten had arrived, and I had five days remaining until my 29th birthday. My brother had went back to Long Beach, and my aunt and unc were still being them. I decided to take me a trip outside of Vegas with the boys for a few days. It was me, Jay and four of his partnas from the gym. Our whole mission was to invade a resort and beat the breaks off of white girls for a few days. You know white girls loved brothers with muscles. More so, they loved this black snake. We caught that quick flight down to Palm Springs, ready to take in everything that was gonna cross our paths.

"Yea!!!" That was Jay screaming as the van from the airport carried us to the Hyatt Resort where we would conduct madness for the next four days.

"A Jay, what's yo plan mane?" He gave me that look like why I was asking him a question that I knew the answer too.

"Man it's only two things on infamous mind. Slay weights and booty meat." The whole van bust out in laughter. Even the shimmy shimmy driver got a good laugh out of it. It was time to live it up for a bit. I knew by the end of these four days that somebody father was gonna be upset at me. We got to the Hyatt safely, checking into our rooms with no qualms. We decided to meet down in the pool area around six, when the temp would start its cool down, and we could enjoy some drinks and chill time. I made a call to my moms back in the D, where she was on her usual scoffing at me for acting up. I swear mothers always treated us like lil kids no matter how old we got. I got down to the pool side cabana we rented out and felt small as fuck. Yea, I was in good shape, but these dudes were some monsters. The shit wasn't fair.

"Man y'all niggas been lifting semi trucks full of smelt all y'all damn life."

"Shit man, you straight. Nigga, we just live in the muthafucka. You visit. Hell as far as I know, a 45 plate opened her pussy and out came me." That was Jay's dude Bruce, but he called him "BANE." He looked just like that nigga too.

"Order these drinks man. Let's get this shit crackin," I told em. Jay called over a bad ass waitress. As she took our orders, that boy was trying the casual flirt approach to see if it was possible to slay those cheeks later. She giggled, knowing that she wanted it. Walking away, I could see that this was gonna be the beginning of one helluva night. Things turnt up quickly all night, as white girl upon white girl joined us at our cabana. Laughing and joking, we were setting the scene for something great and very wild. Time passed quickly. By ten o'clock, we were all in the jacuzzi, beautiful women all over us. Listening to Jay Hall stories of lies was the most hilarious shit ever. He beat into their head that he was a master ninja. Why did they believe that, don't ask me. All I know is that they fell for it hook, line and sinker. It was 10:19 on the dot when I checked my watch. We were all beyond faded, but we were still conscious of what we were doing.

"Hear ye, hear ye," Jay got to yellin. "I hereby give this toast to all this fine ass in this water and all the homies who gone share in it." After busting out laughing, we raised our full glasses of champagne, toasting to the good life. Then that's when we heard it. The scream was loud and eerie. We looked up to a woman falling fast to the concrete. As she made impact, her head split open, splattering blood everywhere. Screams filled the pool side area. Folks started to pull themselves out and run back inside. The girls in the jacuzzi with us all scattered. As for us, we were stunned silent, sitting in the water, not knowing what to make of this. Looking up, I could see a man standing outside on one of the upper floors.

"Virginia, I'm sorry!!! Virginia, I'm sorry!!!," he kept yelling. This wasn't random. This was cold blooded murder. It was like the liquor dissipated out of our blood streams. We were sober and stunned. In that moment, our vacation went to shit. We didn't leave. We all just sat on the edge of the jacuzzi, waiting for authorities to come here. Truthfully, I don't think none of us wanted to move out of fear of our own lives. I mean, this was Palm Springs, old retirement city, full of white folks. We didn't wanna be the next black men on CNN gettin gunned down for being in the right place at the wrong time. Ten minutes passed and noises of sirens filled the air. One by one, police filed into the poolside area, securing the scene with caution tape. From what we seen, they were on one of the upper floors arresting the gentlemen who threw her to her death. He kept screaming he was sorry, but they weren't trying to hear it.

"Gentlemen, this is a crime scene and I am going to need you all to go inside. Furthermore, I understand you are witnesses, correct?" We all nodded in agreement, clearly still distraught. "Well we just wanna ask you guys a few questions about what you saw. Will you follow me please?"

One by one we exited. I was the last one out the bunch. Before I passed into the hotel, I caught an up close glimpse of the corpse right before they threw the sheet over her. Through her blood stained hair and face, I locked eyes with hers, as they were stuck in the open position on the side of her head that was still somewhat recognizable. It was the eeriest shit I had ever seen in my life. It was like she was trying to tell me to save her. I froze for an instance, just gazing at this corpse. As they placed the sheet over her, an officer placed his hand on my back.

"C'mon sir. You have seen enough for one night." I was escorted over to an office where my partnas were. With the way everyone was in here, you would have sworn that our best friend had died. They asked the questions, we all said the same stuff. They already had their suspect, so we weren't worried about them thinking we had did it. We were just worried about how we would go on. After about 30 minutes, we were let go. No one said anything when we walked out of there. We all just went to our separate rooms and chilled for the night. I plopped on my bed, looking over to the clock and seeing that it was ten past twelve.

How could this bad shit happen on such a good damn day? I lied there on top of the sheets, staring into the darkness, the light from the moon shining through my curtains the only illumination inside of my suite. I couldn't fathom how a trip home could have this many twist and turns to it. First, I meet my brother, which I almost stalled on because of pride. Then, there was some serious wrath inside of a man to throw a woman off a hotel balcony. There was the lust me and my partnas had for these random women that we had run into. There was gluttony with our liquor consumption. In ten days, this had turned from a summer of fun, into a summer of sin. My soul felt incomplete. I felt like less of a man. This wasn't who God made me, nor was it the person that he wanted me to be. I had some serious re-evaluating to do. What's funny is how liquor and a tragic incident can always make you rethink your situation. It's like the empty bottle becomes your best friend. You feel as if you can refill it with your problems and pour them out on the concrete as if you were giving a tribute to one of your dead homies. If only it were that easy. I wanted to write, but it wasn't in me. I wanted to sing a song, but it wasn't in me. I wanted to go for a walk, but it wasn't in me. Truth be told, I didn't feel like life was inside of me at all. Vacation wasn't supposed to be like this. It was supposed to be lively, full of joy and life. This felt like I was dead inside, and I wasn't even the one who died tonight. There was a knock at my door. I ignored it. Again, there was a series of knocks.

"LAMAR!!!," I heard whoever it was shout my name. As I got to the door, the police type knocks began.

"AIGHT NIGGA!!!," I told 'em. I opened the door to Jay Hall standing there.

"Man what the fuck are you doing bruh?" I just walked back in the room, trying to ignore bruh. "Lamar, are you seriously gonna mope around here like it was our fault forever?"

"JAY I DON'T WANNA HEAR THIS SHIT BRUH!!!" My breathing was deep and my look intense. What did he do you ask? He laughed. He sat there and just laughed.

"What's funny?"

"You man. Look at you. Stressing over a death you had nothing to deal with." He walked in and shut the door. "Oh sure, we all were fucked up. True dat. The minute I walked back in my room, I got on the phone. I called mama in 'Bama. I told her about it. Got it off my chest. It was over and done with. I went to everyone else's room and nothing. No one wanted to continue what we came here to do and that's have a good time. One very valuable lesson I learned in life was from my damn dog. Yes, my wiener dog Justin. One day, he did the unthinkable and took a shit on the floor. Now Justin usually good about going outside. But that day, he took a shit on the floor. I smelled it, shook my head and cleaned it up."

"So what's the lesson in that?," I asked.

"The lesson is shit happens. Anywhere at anytime. You can either clean it up and move on with life or…..or you can let it sit, stank up your shit some more and just bask in it, complaining about the smell. Now BANE is staying. The other three are leaving. That's their choice. Now you can join them or you can stay. Move on, have your fun and kick life dead square in its ass when it gets tough. Now you make the decision." I pondered his words. First Puncho, now Jay. I was intense, while Jay had a smirk on his face like whatever.

"You don't feel any remorse bruh?" I asked him seriously.

"Look man, we black. You think half of America feels remorse every time one of us is killed? I mean shit, look at what happened in the elevator earlier with us. Those white folks seen your tattoos and got quiet. They asked you what you do sarcastic as shit. When you told em you work systems for the military overseas, you instantly went from nigger invading nice whitey land to Lord and Savior Jesus Christ who rose from the dead on the third day. You see how that shit works? You think we deserve that shit? Lemme answer that. **FUCK NO!!!** So the way I see it, what happened tonight was tragic indeed. However, I'm here to enjoy myself. Had that been one of us, it would have been a sad sight, but folks would've been over that in five minutes. Now, what in the good hell is Lamar gonna do, because Jay is ready to go out and murk the town like a crazy Alabamian." I just shook my head in disbelief. My boy had set me straight once again.

"Man bruh, forgive me for getting emotional. Let's do it."

"Man fuck the apologies," Jay holla'd. "It's past 12. Let's go find some shit to eat man. I gotta get my macros in. Tomorrow it's business as usual." As we exited my room, still in my swimwear and a spare tee, I felt I got my mojo back. I didn't look at things from Jay's perspective. He hit the nail on the head, though. It wasn't necessarily not feeling sad for the young lady who lost her life, but it was the lesson in me learning to keep pushing, even when times were hard. We jumped in the whip and kept it simple, heading over to Denny's for some pancakes. It was amazing how food with a true friend could just settle you down. We jumped shit off the next three days, mobbin hard with two a day workouts and nighttime clubbin'. The days were short, but our nights were long. We didn't come in before four in the morning on each day. Six came, but only three survived. That was just how we were built. Even though I almost faltered, almost doesn't count. It ended up being a damn blast. Even the plane ride back on the 15th was special, as people really thought we were pro bodybuilders or some shit. Man, I couldn't wait for the 16th. 29 was on the way and I was ready to get it in.

The plan was set as nine o'clock rolled around. My mama called me to wish me a happy birthday, along with asking a million questions about what I was doing. The shit was cool falling on a weekend, so it made it even more special.

"Where you headed tonight???," my aunt asked, chillin with my uncle and two of their friends playin' tunk.

"I'm hitting TAO tonight. Gone see how many women drool over your nephew."

"Nigga please," as she slapped another card to the table.

"Bring ya uncle back some sideways nephew." My aunt just looked at him with a menacing stare.

"What baby?," unc said, giggling hard.

"You know what nigga!" The shit was just funny how they reacted with each other. I stepped out the house clean. Vest, tie, jeans and some Stacy's on my feet. I swear I would have a dead man in a casket jealous of me. I jumped in my rental and peeled out into the night. Thank God for connections, cause it ain't no way in hell I would've paid full price for 30 days in a rental. I had V.I.P. access at the club, so the term long ass line didn't even apply to me. I was cruisin', vibin' to some old Domino. Shit seemed in line for the night. Then, as

I exited Tropicana, I had a major revelation at the red light. It seemed longer than usual, and my mindset shifted. Is this what I really wanted to do? Partying with a bunch of randoms was great, but this was home and I had not been here in a year. More importantly, my family hadn't seen me in a year. I turned on green and headed back to the 15 north upon the next turn. I drove all the way back to North Las Vegas. I stopped in the same liquor store where I almost met my demise at a year ago and picked up some Alize and Hennessy. With that, I pulled back up in front of my aunt's crib. I slammed the car door with authority like I was the fucking Godfather. I put the key in the door and walked in a house like I had never did before.

"What you doing back here?," auntie asked.

"Auntie, unc, I been gone over a year. I done partied with everyone and they momma except my own peoples. Everything y'all done for me, it ain't no better way I can think to break in my 29th than to spend it with y'all." I held up the bottle of Alize and Henn. The game stopped briefly.

"Well pour me and Barry a drank and get over here." I happily obliged. With Puddles at my feet, I poured up, getting ready to celebrate yet another year on this Earth.

"You want some baby?," I asked that runt of a dog. Puddles just gave me a blank look. I should've poured some in her bowl and let her get doggie drunk. I brought them their drinks and pulled up a chair. For the next two and a half hours, we didn't even move unless it was to use the bathroom or get some more food or drink. Talk was beyond crazy as everyone was spewing liquor words, curse words and wild ass statements in general. Puddles even started barking a few times, saying her own shit that none of us understood. I was full by 11:50. Henn and chicken wings were doing the most on my soul. My liver had become pissed at me and told me that it would not function for the next couple of days.

"Nephew," unc slurred. "You got ten minutes. What's significant about 29 for you?" Everyone got quiet, waiting for me to answer.

"Well…."as I sipped me some more of my Henn Dog medicine. "All I look forward to is using my time overseas to become a better man and come back here as a redefined individual." Things remained quiet as I finished off the glass.

"Nephew," unc boasted. "Fuck it. Do it. Make yourself the best damn man you can ever be. Just remember one thing. If a motherfucker ever try to kill you, look him in his eyes. Let 'em know you gone snatch his soul to hell upon your demise." Yea, unc was definitely faded beyond belief.

"Barry shut yo ass up," aunt responded back. He ain't even hear it as he fell asleep right there sitting up. We just continued on playing throughout the night. The next time I looked up at the clock, it was 1:02 a.m., August 16, 2013. By now, the friends were gone. Unc and auntie had stumbled to their room and I was just sitting at the table in my own zone. As I poured my last bit of liquor, I looked up and seen the picture of my grandmother on the wall. She was so beautiful inside and out. I raised my glass to her pic.

"I hope I made you proud," I whispered. "I love you Grandma." I didn't even go off to my room. I cut all the lights off and slept right on the couch under her pic. As I faded off into the darkness, I heard something rattle on the floor of the kitchen. It was nothing too loud to alarm me of danger, but I decided to get up and see what it was. After hitting my damn toe on one of the dining room chairs and saying many words of encouragement, I made it to the kitchen light switch. I cut it on, looking around, seeing nothing. Then, I turned around directly behind me. Right where the hardwood met the carpet, I saw two red dice. One rolled six and the other rolled one, just like the one and the six in my birth date. I slowly bent down and picked them both up, shaking them up in my hand. I rolled them back on the hardwood floor. Snake eyes, like two eyes were looking at me. I looked back up at my grandmother's picture. Her eyes looked like they were piercing through my flesh and staring straight into my heart. I wanted to cry, but those days were over. I had cried enough when she died and I know she didn't want that. Her life was to be celebrated, not mourned. I did enough of that in the D. I rolled the dice in my hand and just smiled.

"I love you Grandma." I cut the light off, slowly making my way back to the couch. I yelled out a loud *"FUCK"* in my head as I stubbed the baby toe against the chair again. After again saying more grateful words on how I enjoyed watching fish swim up shit's creek, I rested on the couch and went into dream mode.

"Happy birthday Lamar," I said to myself. "Happy mother fucking birthday my nigga."

The last day before I flew out had arrived and I was more than satisfied. The vacation was more than gratifying. I met my long lost brother who I was now in contact with on a permanent basis. I was reinvented through the death of one person and the friendship of another. My birthday was spent with those who were closest to me. Also, I purchased my first home out in Henderson, solidifying a dream of mine, which was ownership. Life was indeed good. Now in the span of 24 hours, I would have to get back to reality. Work, Work, Work all until next May, when I would hop back on a plane to Vegas for the last time and never see Guam again. That morning, I got up early to meet with Jay at LVAC for a boss type slaughter session. It would be the last time we would kick it before I headed back.

"A bruh, I know what you did for me. I appreciate it much." He stopped dead in the middle of his bench press, holding up 315 like it was a pillow. Re-racking, he sat up and gazed at me.

"The minute I knew he was your brother was the minute that changed me as a man. Whatchu mean Jay you ask? It's simple. When you set your mind to something, you achieve it. You picture it, then you sculpt out what you want until you get the product you desire. You remember when I first went to that body building seminar in LA? I couldn't tell you shit about physique, posing, none of that. All I knew is that when I said I would commit myself to this lifestyle, I was gonna go all in. The minute I gave him your number, he made that choice to go all out to find his long lost brother. That's what life is. A long ass time of decisions. The life part....it's easy. It's the decisions that we make that are hard." He laid back down on that bench to finish out the last six reps he didn't complete previously. It was gone suck leaving a real ass friend because I can't say that about a lot of people. We went on for about another 30 minutes before I showered up and headed out.

"HEY LAMAR!!!," Jay yelled from the gym door as I was getting into my whip.

"SUP BRO!!!???"

"REMEMBER TO GET THOSE GAINZ OUT THERE!!! DON'T GO BACK AND GET LAZY AS SHIT!!!" He walked back in, disappearing from sight. I got in the car, pondering those words. Don't go back and get lazy as shit. Dude was right. With less than a year left, I couldn't get comfortable. I had to keep moving to make my life more than worthwhile. Time flew throughout the day. Before I knew it, 6:45 had rolled around and the sun was beginning its descent into its regular graveyard. To end this vacation on a high note, I swung through Red Rock to catch a view of everything. As I stood on the trails, I amazed and clamored at the beautiful red colored mountains and the shadow being cast upon them by the setting sun. It was like I was the mountains and the sun was setting on my life. I was leaving Vegas a different man from when I came back 28 days ago. In one sense, it was the greatest thing ever. In another, it was scary as ever. It made me think of how the last time I went and visited the D. I had left there changed in more ways than one. I was kind of cold and heartless then. Cuz was murdered right there in front of me. It's hard trying to decipher that shit out of your mental. Just like the shit you went through as a child that you could never fathom. I closed my eyes and faced a demon that I never let go of.

10 GOING HOME

Childhood was a wild one for me. Let me just forget all of the inner city shit. People know about that all too often. From Chicago, Detroit, Compton, Memphis, Birmingham, it's all the same. The plagues that face one hood plague another, however, the trials that plague a child are much more hidden in society. Too often we look at Kanye, Floyd, someone of that stature and assume everything was all peaches and cream, not knowing the true story behind what got them where they are today.

Minus the amounts of money those guys have in their possession, my struggle was no different. The only difference is my biggest struggle wasn't on the city blocks of my hood. My biggest struggle came within the four walls I lived in for eighteen years. All I could do was imagine how many arguments I came home to. The nights I wanted to chill after football practice at Finney, but I couldn't. My parents were steady going back and forth. It never failed. My mom, she was upset at my dad's cheating ways. He had been doing it for the longest and it wasn't any secret. You know it's crazy they say kids see what you don't expect and that is very true. I am the perfect example. I paid attention a lot to how pops moved. How he talked on the phone at times. Yea, I knew some shit was up, but I was too young to understand the game. I felt something wrong in my heart, but I was more concerned about my innocence. All I wanted to do was be a normal child doing normal things. For the most part, I did that. Playing in the park, riding my bike, acting goofy with my friends on their front porch. Life gave me that. But ask yourself this. How can you truly enjoy life outside, when the inside is torn apart? For me, it was my spirit and my home. I dare not sit here and just talk about my pops. I mean, he did his fair share of foul shit, but my mom was far from a saint.

Her anger for her situation was usually taken out on me in the worse ways. At times, the frustration in her voice made me feel terrible, even though I wasn't the intended target. When I was though, it was in the worst way. I can't remember the exact day, time or what I was watching. I was nine years old. Moms was on the couch and I was on the floor locked onto the tube. I think she asked me to do something. I really don't remember. I turned around and gave her my response. I don't think it was a smart response, but however I responded, she didn't like it. Right then, things went in slow motion as she picked up the house phone and launched it towards me.

Unable to move out of the way, it struck me dead in the center of my chest, causing pain beyond belief. I wanted to cry, but the shock and awe factor prevented tears from flowing. I didn't know what to think. All I do know is as I lay down to sleep in my bed that night, my arrhythmia started. I didn't exactly know what was going on, but I knew that my heart wasn't supposed to be beating like that. It was as if my new rhythm wasn't caused by the phone blow. Instead, it was caused by a literal broken heart. My parents didn't get along, and I was feeling the wrath, whether that be physically or emotionally. I will never forget that night. It started more than a lifetime of heart ailments, but also a lifetime of internalized pain that took me a long time to get over. Come to think about it, the worst part of everything for me was wondering why was I even born. It seemed like everything revolved around Lamar. I just sometimes wished they didn't have me or that I was born into a rich family so I wouldn't have to deal with this nonsense. I endured this trial and pain for eighteen years.

My grandmother saved my life, though. She was like that best friend that you could always run to when things got rough. I don't know how many times I cried to her on nights just wishing something different would happen in my life. I was tired. I felt like an elder statesman instead of a young child. With the stress my parents put me through, I should have been the one with grey hair and wrinkles. When I was 13, I severely thought about suicide. When my parents were busy or just not home, I would sit under the doorknob of my closet door. I'd take my pants belt and wrap it around my neck. I would then buckle it up to the last hole possible. My neck was much smaller back then, so it was easy to get a good grip, however, it wasn't good enough for me. I wanted to feel my breath leaving my body. I started to say skip the holes, just wrap it around the knob and pull the ends until I choked like someone was trying to have a death grip on my throat. I don't know how many times I did that, but if I had a nickel for every time I felt that rush of life leaving, I would've been ballin' for a thirteen year old.

That was eighth grade year, and more than that had occurred. I failed my last hour class, simply for the fact that I couldn't concentrate because I was more concerned about what I was going to deal with at home. The shit was like night and day. Jekyll and Hyde. I could go home one day and everything was peaches and cream. The next, it was hell in a blue house. I sometimes felt that the devil was sitting on the couch watching my parents go at each others throats. I thought he was sympathetic. I thought the devil would say, 'Man, he can't chill with me for eternity. His folks are putting him through more strife and grief than I could ever do.' Times were just down right dirty. When I was 14, my parents separated for a good minute. I hated going back and forth. Some nights, staying with my moms. Other nights, staying with my dad. I more so hated staying with my mom due to the simple fact that she stayed over in the Mexican hood. I had nothing personal against them, but the way they got down in the hood, I wasn't feeling it. I was on pins and needles every time I would walk anywhere over there. Staying with pops was much easier, but it was also much more tense as well. No time became more tense than when his side piece came to the door. I had answered a few of her calls before when she hit the line of the house. I knew it wasn't our "cousin" as he so often proclaimed. Any who, she came to the door, asking for him. I didn't look at her strange, but in the back of my mind, I was pissed. I went and got pops from the room, telling him someone was at the door. I left things alone, going to my room until I decided to get curious. I looked out the porch window. There he was, outside by the car, looking like the convo had taken a serious tone. When it was all said and done, he came back in the house.

"Was that Jazzy?," I asked him.

"Nah Nah," as he walked it back quickly to the bedroom. I knew he was lying. He knew he was lying. What I think hurt him the most is that he knew I knew. I may have only been 14, but I wasn't the dumb little boy anymore. I wasn't seven anymore. There wasn't any maybe's or if's. There was certainty that I knew because I was a lot older and I was up on game. His favorite line to tell me was always 'that you can't bullshit a bullshitter.' He had forgot that he had taught me a lot of bullshit and he couldn't bullshit me. That's not even the half of it really.

Time went on, and eventually, they got back together. Things were actually cool for a little while. When I say lil', I really mean lil'. That's why I stayed so active in sports. In the fall, it was football. In the winter, it was basketball. In the spring, it was track. I wrestled one year for a bit. After getting my ass kicked the first time on the mat, I was done. A nigga was ready to fight. It was one thing to mess up on the football field with 21 other people. In wrestling though, it was one on one, and when you caught an ass whoopin', everybody seen it.

I stayed active, not for the love of sports, but did it simply to stay up out of the house. My homework got done while I was in school. When I got home from practice, it was at least eight o'clock or later. All I had to do was come in, eat, watch some TV in my room and go to sleep. The least amount of time I had with my parents, the better off I felt. Times were just a waste for me. My getaways were simply me in my own space, in my own zone. I dibbled dabbled in poetry back then, but it wasn't for freedom of the mind. Now looking back at it, I kind of wished I saw that gift back then. It would have been a better release instead of drinking with my friends in their basements, or smoking weed on the corner with some of my dawgs before school. That shit kept me away from the world I was living in. More importantly, it kept me away from my true self.

One thing I did realize from going through what I went through was that I had the strength to endure any and everything possibly thrown at me. People can survive bullets, car accidents, falls and all sorts of other catastrophes. To survive a home without love as a child, you definitely can conquer anything you face as a grown individual. I sat well past the sunset on that trail. My journey had been conquered. I thought Guam was my bread and butter. The obstacle that would define my life. I realized that my entire childhood and the parents whom I once had hated, made me the man I am today. My love for them may have been weary, but their misdeeds towards each other are what made Lamar Atteley III successful.

To Mom and Dad. Thank you.

CATFISH AND GRITS

One day I got hungry and cooked me some Catfish & Grits.....I mean it's a quick meal, a nice fill...and it's truly a ghetto classic...as I poured the grits into the semi boilin' water though, I watched em like never before.....see I started to realize that life was a lot like cookin' catfish and grits. See, as the grits got thicker it reminded me of my skin, the same way it thickened up to take hatred, criticism, and the occasional nigga I encountered when visitin' Southern states, and gettin' loose and out of character was represented when they were stirred, the same way life can stir up your emotions and make you forget your purpose....See catfish brought me back to reality, cause much like that fish, life is nasty, taking in any and everything, just to turn around and get consumed by us, but we don't wanna taste life sometimes, so we doctor it up with seasonings and marinades, drop that thang in the fryer and watch it burn crisp, just like in life when we try to get rid of our own personal ish, we burn others in the process, cause much like frying, life is simple, you don't have to be a genius to get thru this, in frying, you drop the meat and wait til it floats to the top, in life, you realize, you start from the bottom and work your way to the top, but now this mindset has been flopped more than the Miami Heat....and we wanna make it to the homes off the highways without first traveling the rugged streets, so maybe we need to get fined 5G's for floppin', cause the mindset nowadays has us stoppin' progression before it even starts........and a dinner plate is nothin' more than mere food instead of a savored dish............see life is now this, a regular meal, no flavor, no savor, just food, enough to fill you up temporarily and the thought of it not changin' is scary so maybe when we have nothin' left to eat but celery and berries, then, and only then, will we once appreciate what life has cooked up for us, so for y'all that don't get this concept, gone and eat it up.

Back here in Guam, we were all gravy, me, Ruby and her young new employee. She kept smiling at me and looking down as young girls do and it was funny as ever. That's the tell tale sign that someone is diggin' you. However, this brother here didn't mess with young girls, especially teens. Unfortunately, I can't say that for all men because some of these fools are beyond perverted. 45 years old and kicking it with middle schoolers as if it were the cool thing to do. We sat there enjoying great laughs. Another open mic had come and gone. Java Hut was closed, but as always, Ruby as a gracious owner, allowed me to stay so that I may learn something and not just talk. Afterwards, I thought I was gonna shoot down to Tumon, maybe step inside the Pentagon for a minute, grace some people with my presence and see if I could come up on something new. The chance of that was rare, but you never knew. I must say this, though, after almost a year and a half on this rock, this place had grown on me. As much as I did wanna leave, there was also a small part of me that wanted to stay. Yea, Guam was special. I would never forget it when I left. The night continued on well past 9:30.

"Oh snaps!!!," Ruby said. "I gotta get home. My husband is probably throwing a fit right now being stuck with the kids."

"Ok Rube. I will be out and about. Until next week."

"Bye Lamar!!!," she said as she was going over the night's earnings. I took one last bite of that fire ass food.

"DON'T NOBODY MAKE A FUCKING MOVE!!!" I stopped dead in mid bite as I looked up to the barrel of a gun in my face. I didn't even hear homeboy come in the joint. **"DON'T TRY AND BE A HERO. GET YO ASS OVER IN THE CORNER!!!"**

I was shook and shaking in my Adidas. Two seconds ago I was having a good vibe, good food and good times. Now we were all stuck in some shit. This behemoth of a man grabbed me by my collar and flung me over to the couch. Ruby was behind the register, along with her young teenage employee, frozen stiff. They were closing down for the night and allowed me to stay in to help them end their night with some great conversation. Now this may have just been our last conversation.

"BITCH, PUT ALL THE MONEY IN THIS BAG!!!" As Ruby tried to get the register open, he slapped her once upside the head. **"HURRY THE FUCK UP!!!"** As my blood boiled, I knew it wasn't much I could do. The couch and where he was standing was a good couple of feet away so I had no chance to jump up and try anything, not to mention I had to get past a table and another chair.

"DON'T MAKE ANY FUCKING MOVE OR YOUR LIFE IS OVER!!!" As he turned back to me, face hiding behind a black ski mask, I realized something. He may have been yelling viciously, but telling by the slight nervousness in his voice, I could tell he didn't want to do this, but I knew that he was desperate and in need of money.

"Here sir," Ruby's young employee mumbled out, trying to maintain the small amount of calmness she had.

"THIS IS IT???!!! THIS IS FUCKING IT???!!!" He struck her with the gun, knocking her out cold. As Ruby ran to the back, I darted towards him. I figured if I was going to die then I was gonna go out fighting. As I neared him, he turned around smoothly and clocked me with the barrel. Down I went, grabbing my forehead in pain.

"FUCK!!!," I yelled out repeatedly as he gave me continuous kicks to my stomach. I knew that the chance of me making it out alive was slim to none now.

"GET YOUR ASS UP!!!," he told me as he snatched and took me to the back towards the kitchen. I was out of it. Blood was pouring from my head as things started to get blurry. "WHERE ARE YOU??," he screamed.

Ruby was nowhere in sight. I know she hadn't ran out and left us, but I damn sure hoped like hell she called the cops. I was drug back behind the counter, where through my blurred vision, I could see babygirl still laid out on the floor unconscious. She couldn't have been no older than 17 or 18. If she made it through this, she would be severely scarred for life. I no longer cared about me. I had lived my life. I could take death, but I couldn't take a young person not even having the chance to begin theirs.

"Just kill me and let them live," I whispered, damn near completely out of it from the loss of blood.. As he drug me to the end of the narrow hall to a small door labeled office, he responded in a way I couldn't even imagine.

"I don't wanna do this, but I have no choice. You're from Detroit. You should know this." How in the fuck? Things had taken a whole new turn now. It's bad enough to lose your life in a robbery, to have lost it to someone you know, or may know, that's the worst of the worst.

"OPEN UP!!! I KNOW YOU'RE IN THERE!!!" He screamed with the pistol pointed directly at my temple. I was powerless and I hated this feeling. He kicked it in and there was Ruby, sitting in the corner, screaming her head off.

"GIMME THE FUCKING PHONE!!!" He threw me in the office and slammed the door.

"The police have been called so leave now while you still can," she barrelled out. He smacked her once more and gave her communication of another level by aiming the nine directly at her temple. "Do you wanna die right here?" Then Ruby began to stand.

"SITDOWN!!!," he screamed. Ruby refused. She was fully on her feet now, dried up blood decorating her lips. The look in her eyes said it all. **"SIT DOWN...OR I SHOOT!!!,"** he holla'd one more time.

"Look motherfucker," she said, with a fire in her eyes. "If you're looking for someone to die on her knees, then you go get a bitch raised on the corner. You kill me...........then you kill a **WOMAN**..........**A WOMAN**...............who stands at death, stares at it, says **FUCK YOU**.......................and bring it. Just know, you kill me, I'll ask God to let me meet you at the Judgement Day gates so I can beat the fire out yo ass. That way, the devil won't have to worry about burning you.......cause I already did." I could now hear cop sirens. They were getting closer and closer. Ruby and this would be tough guy had a stare down for the ages. He was shook I know.

"I'm sorry Ruby," he uttered.

POP!!! He blasted her with a quick shot to the head. Ruby's blood splattered my body and the surrounding walls. At the same time, I heard the police storm through the front door.

POP, POP, POP!!! Three shots to my body. I wasn't dead, but bullets were burning the life out of me slowly. Two in my leg and one in my stomach. In an instance, he took off his mask. Puncho. Puncho. It was fucking Puncho!!!

You know that moment where time sits still and doesn't move? Well..........this was it. Time went back to our functions throughout our time here. The first initial meeting. The New Year's Eve bash where we partied like it was 1999 instead of 2012. The yacht parties where we popped bottles and just had a wild time with the ladies of Guam. The knowledge passing sessions at the table of extraordinary gentlemen as I would call it, where we would uplift each other while challenging each other to expand our mindsets and become greater men than what we already were. All this was washed down the drain. It wasn't as bad as Peter denying Jesus, but it was in the aspect of two hood niggas who linked up and made their situations better than what they were before we met. You think you know people, but they only allow you to see what they really want you to see. It's much like many highly visible figures of this Earth.

You ever have someone make it from your hometown, but you swear they don't give back because you never see the fruits of their labor blossoming in your city? Well, who is to say that they haven't given back all because YOU as an individual have not seen it? The greatest way to give back to whatever city you are from is to leave it and go make it somewhere else. How are you gonna rep your city if you never left your city? Go somewhere else and make it and that's how you help your city. That's the beauty of not knowing a person fully. In this case however, it was my worse nightmare.

"W-W-Why P??," I mumbled out my mouth that was full of blood. With tears in his eyes, he said a statement that soaked into the mind of my dying frame.

"Sometimes extraordinary men become basic in the mind." Letting out a scream, he flung the door open, pointing the gun towards the door. All I seen was his body get riddled with bullets as he fell over, gun falling with him. Struggling for air, I reached in my pocket and grabbed a piece of paper. I managed to get it open even in my disoriented state. It was 'REGRET', the first poem I ever wrote.

"We got a stiff and one still alive!!! Get medics in here immediately!!!" I faintly remember anything but lights. I was slippin' and felt the life leaving me slowly, but surely. I thought this would happen to me growing up in the D. Instead, I was taking my last breaths on the G. On the G. On the G. To many, that's a solidifying phrase. For me, it was my final resting place. The voices of the EMT's and the sirens of the ambulance were a new tune my ears weren't ready for.

"Please God, forgive me for all of my sins," I asked Him. I wasn't sure if I was good with God before, but I was hoping that little phrase would have Him forgive me fully.

"He will, Son. He is a merciful God, but you'll be okay." I don't know what medic said it, nor did I see him because everything was blurry. I did however, believe him.

"We're losing him, we have to hurry up." I didn't even realize I made it to the hospital. My eyes only seen white and blue. Hands were everywhere. Then I lost sense of everything around me.

"Stay with us Lamar. Stay with us. **I need more blood!!!**," the doc yelled out. I was starting to see visions of both of my grandmothers. My granddad that had passed my senior year of high school. I was seeing all of my niggas who lost their lives in the street. Dino, Jamie, Ray, Leonard, Darryl, all of em. The craziest one of em all is when I seen my cousin Pooh. I seen a vision of him just staring at me. They had killed my cousin execution style. Twenty four shots. They didn't have to do him like that. I knew my time was on its way. I was just trying to hold on. As I faded in and out, I could hear chatter from the docs, but couldn't make out what they were doing to me. It was like I was sleeping with the lights on. I was trying to rest, and yet stay alive at the same time.

"LAMAR!!! LAMAR!!! YOU STILL WITH US!!! LAMAR!!!....................................."

"WHOA SHIT!!!!" I screamed as I shot up. I woke up shaking, sweating and scared shitless. My breathing was intense and deep. You would've swore I was losing my virginity instead of taking a Friday afternoon nap. I was so out of it that I didn't even hear my phone ringing. I reached over to look at my screen and seen it was Tony, one of my co-workers.

Me: "What's good man?"

Tony: "Bruh, I'm gone get straight to the point. You been busting your ass for a long time now and folks see that. Recently, something came up, boss man asked my opinion on it and I said I got the perfect person for this opportunity."

I sat up on the edge of my bed, fully focused now on this convo. "Go on T."

"Aight look. It's a position as a head intel analyst overseas. The position is just for two years, but it can propel you even higher if you take it." Inside I was saying hell yeah.

"Where would I be living bruh?," I asked him.

"Guam homey. You'd be going to Guam."

"I'm down bruh. Let's do it."

"You sure you wanna do this man? I mean….this ain't just moving somewhere else across the states. You risking it all to move halfway across the world. In a whole different world for that matter." I sat there and pondered this question for what seemed like eternity.

"Gimme some time to think about it bruh………"

ABOUT THE AUTHOR

Joe McClain Jr. was born and raised in the Harborside section of East Chicago, Indiana. After graduating from East Chicago Central High School in 2002, he enlisted in the United States Navy and relocated to San Diego, California. He has been to nineteen countries to include Spain, Italy, Dubai, Guam and The Philippines. He authored his first book, "The Writer's Block", in 2013 and followed it up with "BANDAGES," released in early 2015. Aside from writing, he is also a well seasoned poet who has shared the stage with numerous def jam artists and has opened for r&b soul artists Dwele, Jon B. and Joe. More can be found on Joe at his website www.joemacucnut.com

IF YOU ENJOYED READING
"SLEEPING WITH THE LIGHTS ON"
PLEASE LEAVE A REVIEW ON AMAZON.COM
http://ow.ly/JggvZ

ALSO AVAILABLE

When his father passed at 12, Mr. Terrelle Washington grew up fast and survived the dangerous streets of East Chicago, Indiana. After finding out his deceased father left him a large inheritance, he decided to leave for California and achieve his dream of becoming a published Author. However, the land of Hollywood stars was soon transformed into a maze of unforeseen obstacles he never expected on his way to the top. How will it play out??? Will he achieve his dream, or will it be shattered into a nightmare of failure.

A hard life in the inner city. Made it through. About to prepare for the next step of most young men. College. That was all until one fateful night to where freedom was taken away. Now, in the battle of his young life, a young man has two options. Die in prison, or snitch and possibly get another chance. Either choice will draw consequences, but what will he choose??? What wounds will be healed, and what wounds will be re-opened???

Ricky Walters grew up in the gritty streets of San Diego California. Upon quitting his security job, he meets an ex pimp name Trust who teaches him everything about the pimp game. Ricky ends up turning out a young Asian girl name Yuki, changes his name to Jackpot, and jumps knee deep in the pimp game. Jackpot makes a conscious decision to become the biggest pimp to ever play the game and goes cross country. Here, is where Jackpot finds himself getting money, ducking the police, feuding with haters, vindictive females, snitches, and eventually doing time in the penitentiary.

Let Me Pimp Or Let Me Die 2, tells the story of a few female workers in the "Game," told through their lives as you see and find out what motivates a woman to start ho'n and sell her body. Re-visit some of your favorite characters from part 1 and see what drove them into the lifestyle that they chose. Each story different but ultimately the same.

Graphic and not for the faint of heart, the scenes take place in a realistic setting with many twist n turns you won't see coming. Find out how F.A.B Killed Sunshine and what happened in those last moments. How Green Eyes got hooked on drugs and the real reason she left Jackpot for dead in prison. Or the number one question...Will Jackpot Return To The Game?

Xavier Sands and Danielle Seville meet at the grand opening of Xavier's nightclub, and it happens to be his birthday. Not to be left out, Danielle is celebrating her birthday as well. As the two grow closer, wedges are driven between them behind the scenes, by their own mothers!

Xavier and Danielle both work for King Kole Konners, in different venues, but when the King is shot, all bets are off. The kingdom having just survived the Chase St. John mutiny in South Nubia, is rocked once again. The assassin begins picking off the King's top people, leading to Danielle being kidnapped.

Xavier vows vengeance on the person, or persons responsible for the shooting of the King. During her kidnapping ordeal, Danielle learns a horrible, life changing secret. Just as her world is rocked, Xavier learns the same shocking truth from his mother.

COMING SOON

"**Freeze mother fucker!**" a cop spat, but the Skyline hardhead wasn't trying to hear it. He blindly reached on the floor for his gun as he slowly regained his eyesight. Jail wasn't an option for the young rida. He knew he had done too much to turn back. Fuck it, he was gonna hold court in the streets. As he placed his hand on the gun that laid dormant on the floor, that would be as close as he got to picking it up and letting off a shot...

THE WRITER'S BLOCK 2
FALL 2015

UPROCK AUDIOBOOKS

Don't have the time to read? Well, we have the solution. Pick up your audio version of "Let Me Pimp Or Let Me Die." The book by Caujuan Akim Mayo that started it all. Listen to this action pack audio book, loaded with special sound effects and cinematic music for dramatic effect, like no other audio book you've ever heard before. This is the audio book, that changed the game and set the bar.

- Website: www.uprockpublications.com
- Emails: uprockp@gmail.com
- Facebook: uprockpublications
- Twitter: uprockpub
- Contact: (619) 259-0298